Union Jacked

"Fashion is always at the forefront, but never at the cost of excellent writing, humorous dialogue, or a compelling story." -*Kings River Life*

"A captivating new mystery voice, Vallere has stitched together haute couture and murder in a stylish mystery. Dirty Laundry has never been so engrossing!" -Krista Davis, *New York Times* Bestselling Author of The Domestic Diva Mysteries

"Samantha Kidd is an engaging amateur sleuth." -*Mysterious Reviews*

"It keeps you at the edge of your seat. I love the description of clothes in this book...if you love fashion, pick this up!" -*Los Angeles Mamma Blog*

"Diane Vallere takes the reader through this cozy mystery with her signature wit and humor." -Mary Marks, *NY Journal of Books*

"The Samantha Kidd Mysteries continue to be completely fun and entertaining." -*Carstairs Considers*

THE KILLER FASHION MYSTERY SERIES

Killer Fashion Mysteries

Designer Dirty Laundry

Buyer, Beware

The Brim Reaper

Some Like It Haute

Grand Theft Retro

Pearls Gone Wild

Cement Stilettos

Panty Raid

Union Jacked

Slay Ride

Tough Luxe

Fahrenheit 501

Stark Raving Mod

Gilt Trip

Ranch Dressing

Murder Italian Style

UNION JACKED: A Killer Fashion Mystery

Book #9 in the Killer Fashion Mystery Series

A Polyester Press Mystery

ISBN: 9781954579088

E-ISBN: 9781954579071

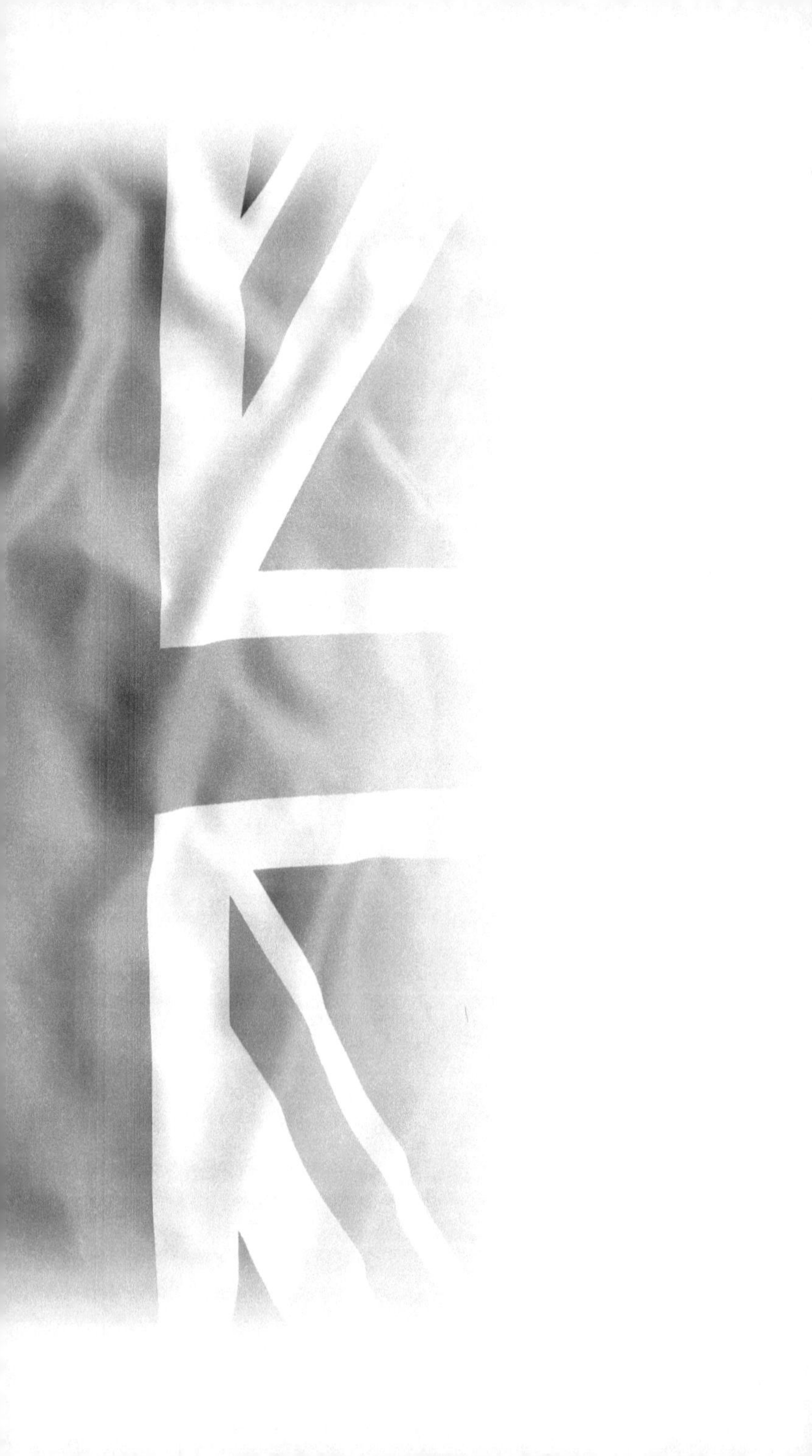

Union Jacked

DIANE VALLERE

For the US Picks

UNION JACKED

1

SIMONTHA

THIS WASN'T my cup of tea. I mean, technically, it *was* my cup of tea. Technically, all eight of the cups on the table were my cups of tea. But I'm more of a coffee person, and if I had to sample any more of the eight corresponding pots of tea on the table, I was going to float away.

"Simontha, it is imperative that you decide quickly," the woman from the British Embassy said. "It's a matter of life and death."

Victoria Pratt, the woman pressuring me to be swift and decisive, wasn't really from the British Embassy. And choosing a flavor of tea wasn't a life-and-death matter. But ever since Nick Taylor, my husband of less than a year, had left for an extended business trip to Asia to outsource a new designer sneaker collection, my active imagination had been given room to run wild. Pretending

Victoria and I were on a mission of some importance helped me focus on the outcome (and ignore the way she said "Samantha").

I sometimes think I would have made an excellent secret agent.

"The blue teapot," I said. "Definitely the blue one."

"English breakfast. Brilliant. Next, we choose scones."

Victoria was the sales executive for Piccadilly Group, a British investment company that had bought Tradava, the department store where I worked. She wore a white shirt under a teal sweater under a tweed blazer over flat-front, camel-colored, narrow-legged pants tucked into riding boots. Her hair was strawberry blond and bobbed at chin length, and her skin was creamy with a touch of pink in the cheeks that looked one hundred percent natural. If I rubbed a magic lantern and conjured up a British sales executive, I couldn't have imagined a better manifestation.

She took her tea very seriously.

I was less interested in the tea selection than I pretended to be. When Victoria heard I was planning a party for—let's call him a colleague—in addition to the grand reopening party for Tradava, she approved my request to host my side party right here. That decision solved the problem of location but left me with the unique challenge of explaining a British-themed retirement party for a homicide detective.

Considering it was a surprise party, I had at least a week to figure something out.

While Victoria poured our next mug of tea, fireworks testing commenced. The bright sun made the display undetectable by sight, but the sound of cannons followed by pops made it impossible to ignore.

Piccadilly Group was the financial savior who had swept in and saved Tradava, the department store where I worked as the buyer of special assortments. (It's a bogus title.) They consolidated our inventory, which we sold off in a clearance sale, and they remerchandised the store into novelty departments based on the whims of their buying team on the other side of the Atlantic. I was assigned to spend the week with their senior sales executive who'd been tasked to train me on the British way of thinking.

How hard could it be? Did they think I've never read *Bridget Jones's Diary?*

The fireworks quieted down, and I flipped a white folder open and pulled out the top sheet of paper. "Victoria, I don't think you've locked in entertainment yet, right? I found a band that could liven things up—"

"Simontha," she said, putting her hand on my upper arm. "You're precious. But remember, this grand reopening is about shopping. We want to offer our customers something they didn't know they needed. If they want to listen to a band, they can go to a pub. Do you understand?" She asked this last question as if I were a small child learning new vocabulary words.

"But this isn't just any band. It's an all-female, punk rock cover band called The—"

"Simontha," she interrupted.

"I understand."

"Brilliant."

While Victoria refreshed her tea (Darjeeling? Oolong?), an attractive man with a swarthy complexion, dark hair, and one-inch sideburns jogged toward us. He wore a hooded sweatshirt under a blazer with well-worn jeans and Converse sneakers. "Hi," he said to me. "You work at the store, right?"

"Yes," I said.

He tossed a folder onto the table next to mine and held out his hand. "Harvey Monahan. I'm the strike leader."

"Kidd," I said. "Samantha Kidd." I shook his hand.

"How come you're not with us?"

"I was needed out here."

Harvey shook his head. "Management is taking advantage of you. Tradava lays off three-quarters of the store staff and thinks everybody will show up for a paycheck. They're working you harder than the law allows. And for what? You deserve a voice."

"My job is interesting. Every day it's something differ-ent." Like six months ago when they sent me to Las Vegas to cover the lingerie market. The trip had ended in a spontaneous wedding ceremony and a honeymoon in Paris. I doubted that would have been in the job description if my job were more official.

"Are you sure everybody wants to be picketing?" I asked. "Some people are probably happy the store isn't going out of business. Maybe they don't want to rock the boat."

Harvey scowled. "They don't know how it works. I've coordinated strikes at retailers from here to New Jersey. Our actions will show Piccadilly Group they can't walk all over us. I have a ninety-nine percent success rate in negotiating for better compensation packages."

"Why not one hundred?"

He waved his hand dismissively. "We got hung up on parking spaces in Cherry Hill." He pulled his phone from his pocket and smiled at something on the screen. "Management is about to cave, and they won't be able to ignore me after today." He winked, and despite my newlywed status, I blushed.

Harvey turned to Victoria. He tapped the folder on the table. "These are for you," he said.

Without stopping, her eyes darted from the biscuits to the shiny white folder and back to the biscuits. "Not necessary." If I hadn't been paying attention, I might not have noticed the faint blush that crept up her neck.

Victoria checked her watch—an expensive-looking timepiece with Roman numerals and a leather strap that wrapped around her wrist several times—and sighed.

"Simontha, I need to pop into the store for a liaison with human resources. Can I trust you to carry on until I return?"

"Sure," I said, though the carrying on part seemed vague since we'd already chosen our tea. "Why don't I follow up on that band I mentioned?"

She gave me a tight-lipped smile. Harvey grabbed his folder from the table, and they walked toward the store. The two of them made an odd pair as they crossed the lot: his dark, Mediterranean good looks and mostly black attire, her peaches-and-cream complexion and English countryside ensemble. Yet I sensed Victoria wasn't inexperienced when it came to negotiations and wondered if Harvey's record was about to take a hit.

I waited until Victoria was out of sight before pulling a bag of pretzels out of my handbag and biting into a loop. My stomach had been queasy all morning, and I figured pretzels were a close cousin to saltines. I chased the pretzel with a swig from a small silver flask filled with coffee.

A dark-blue sedan pulled into the parking lot. The car stopped in front of me, and my favorite homicide detective got out. (What? Don't you have a favorite homicide detective too?) I quickly capped my flask and hid it behind me.

"Detective Loncar," I said. I considered asking what brought him there but was afraid to jinx any possible interest in him updating his wardrobe.

Detective Loncar and I had an interesting past. He was in his mid-sixties, wore ill-fitting suits, was going through a divorce, and investigated homicides around Ribbon. I'd say he's the person I'd call if I ever got arrested, but the more likely situation is that he'd already be there.

This was bad. This was worse than bad. Not because it may have appeared to the detective that I was day-drinking in the open parking lot outside my employer, but because in addition to my job responsibilities, I had a secondary secret agenda.

"I'm organizing the grand reopening for Tradava," I said tentatively. "There are a lot of decisions to be made. Decisions that require my unique knowledge of, um, stuff."

Loncar crossed his arms. "Are your plans going to cause problems that could tax the police department resources unnecessarily?"

"This party is as much for you as it is for them," I said without thinking.

Loncar's expression changed from mildly tolerant to understanding. And in this case, understanding translated to a probably correct—let's face it; he was a detective—suspicion of what I meant.

"You're not—"

I winced. "I am."

He shook his head. "I don't believe this."

"Just to be clear, what do *you* think I'm doing here?"

"Ms. Kidd," he said. The people on the other side of the parking lot could probably sense his annoyance.

"Right. Technically, I *am* out here working for Trada-va." Oh, bloody hell. "But I'm planning your retirement party too."

2

ABOVE YOUR PAY GRADE

IN THE THREE years that I'd been in Ribbon, Loncar and I had moved into comfortable territory. He was among the first three phone calls I made when I stumbled onto something suspicious, and I was—well, I wasn't sure what I was to him. Hey! Maybe I was his informant! *(Get PoPT!* says it's important to claim credit for our contributions to the world around us. I wonder if I should add "informant" to my LinkedIn profile?) But now, the detective was facing mandatory retirement from the force.

There were approximately thirteen hundred reasons why I shouldn't have known that. Despite my proclamations to the contrary, Loncar and I weren't friends. He was a cop, and I was a resident in his city. A resident who, some might say, made his job more difficult. Not me, though. To me, we're practically partners.

But word trickled through the community: from a

couple of cops to the local crime reporter for the *Ribbon Times* to a hair stylist at the salon next to my store to the cashier working the candy counter where I occasionally treated myself to a couple of dark chocolate peanut clusters before driving home to me. And when the police captain reached out to ask me to coordinate the party, the most convoluted version of whisper down the alley came to an end.

Captain Valderama hadn't asked Loncar's ex-wife.

Or his daughter.

Or his partner.

Not even a discount party planner.

He asked me.

I recognized the possibility that a joke was being made at Loncar's expense and instead of being in on it, I was part of it. Which was why I was determined to take the party seriously.

I had no intention of filling Detective Loncar in on the plans for his party. I also had no plans to run with the obvious cop theme. (I'd recently found myself participating in a cop-themed fashion show at a lingerie fair and blushed at the idea of recreating it for the local police force.)

But to plan a party, I needed a theme.

To use Tradava's resources, I needed a British theme.

I started thinking about everything I'd learned about the detective from my research. Who was he? Not the cop.

Not the father. Not the husband. But him? The man under the ill-fitting suit?

I don't mean like *that*.

Within minutes of hanging up from Captain Valderama, I'd discovered the history of the Loncar surname in Ribbon, Pennsylvania. (Twenty percent of the world's Loncars occupied Pennsylvania in 1920, and I'd briefly flirted with a flapper theme.)

A call to Loncar's daughter provided slightly more information: his ancestors had come here from the UK in 1841 with the first Loncars, and his great-great-grandfather, who'd been a baby on that trip, had grown up and fought for the union in the battle of Gettysburg. (I'd briefly flirted with a Civil War theme.)

But it wasn't the war, or the era, or the lack of inspiration from the events in Loncar's family history that provided the theme. It was something far more personal, something unbelievably informative about the man Detective Loncar had once been.

It was a Spice Girls ticket stub from 1996.

I called Loncar's daughter and asked if it was hers. "No," she'd said with a laugh. "That's a joke in our family. My dad has a thing for Ginger Spice. It's where I got my name. Mom took him to a concert for his forty-fifth birthday. She said she never saw him as happy as he was that night." (Now that she'd sent him divorce papers, I briefly considered reaching out to Geri Halliwell to coordinate an introduction, but sadly for Loncar, she appeared to be happily married.)

I found my British theme.

Would Detective Loncar appreciate my efforts? I didn't know. But since it was technically a surprise party, I wasn't supposed to have to deal with that until the day of the surprise.

Figures Loncar was a spoilsport.

Loncar turned away from Tradava and scanned the teapots, mugs, and biscuits. He reached for the folder that contained my notes on the party, and I slid it out of his reach. I gave him my most charming smile. "Above your pay grade."

"Hear me out," I said. "I know you. I know you don't want this party. That makes me the best person to plan it. I won't embarrass you. I won't let anybody turn it into a joke. I even convinced Tradava to let me use their party set-up, and Eddie is going to help with execution, so anybody who isn't invited will think it's part of the grand reopening."

Loncar was temporarily distracted. He looked at the department store for a moment. "Will it help the store?"

I should have been surprised by the question, but I wasn't.

"Hard to say," I said. I stared at the façade of the store too. "Business has been tough, but Tradava doesn't want to publicize that. It's like they went through a bad breakup and nobody wants to date them, but they keep on putting on lipstick anyway."

Loncar furrowed his brow at my analogy.

"You think the British invasion is the answer?"

"Piccadilly's money could ensure the store continues, but it won't be the Tradava people know and love. The days of shopping for fishing gear and prom dresses under the same roof are numbered." I didn't add that to me, that signified an upgrade. "We'll lose what makes the store unique to Ribbon."

Loncar turned back. He appeared to notice the flask I'd tried to conceal. "Coffee," I said. I unscrewed the cap and held the flask toward him as evidence.

He waved it off. "What can you tell me about the strike?"

"Not much. Last week The Piccadilly Group downgraded the support divisions to hourly, and the local retailer's union brought in a captain to organize a walkout. He said they needed to strike while the iron was hot or they'd never get respect from the new owners."

Loncar kept his eyes on me but didn't speak.

"Strike while the iron is hot," I repeated. "That's funny in the context of Tradava being a clothing store. You know, irons?" I pantomimed ironing something. "Get it? They're hot when you plug them in to iron things? Although, I don't think that's what the union captain meant, unless he's funny too, and I don't know if he's funny. Union captains aren't supposed to be funny, are they? But he did say 'strike.' Do you think he intended the pun?"

Loncar shook his head.

A fresh round of fireworks fired. Loncar put his hand over his ear and whacked it a few times with his palm. "Were fireworks your idea?"

"No. I wanted to charter a biplane with a banner that said, 'Loncar Retires! Round up the usual suspects.'"

Loncar shook his head. "No party."

I jabbed my finger close enough to his chest to make my point while not assaulting a police officer. "This party isn't for you," I said. "It's for your department. And your daughter. And the employees of the store who thought they were going to be out of a job. And the city of Ribbon who want to celebrate your career."

"I want to approve everything from the invitees to the color of the icing on the cupcakes."

"Who said there would be cupcakes? Do you want cupcakes? I was thinking donuts. Do you *like* cupcakes?"

"No donuts. Nothing that mocks the department. Just do what you're going to do and keep me posted."

Like I said: practically partners!

———

LONCAR APPROACHED THE PICKETERS, and I finished my flask of coffee. I taste-tested three biscuits and called in an order for fish and chips to number six on Yelp's list of

Best British Food in Ribbon. The picketers appeared to be on a break. My phone rang. The name of my close friend and adjacent picketer Eddie Adams flashed on the screen, and I answered.

"Coffee. Black. Blacker than black. How black? None more black."

Since Piccadilly had announced their plans to buy out Tradava and assort us with British merchandise, Eddie had taken to talking like Christopher Guest's character from *This Is Spinal Tap.* You might think a Pennsylvanian surfer dude can't pull off an East London accent. You'd be right. (I kept my opinion to myself.)

"I can't leave for coffee. Moneypenny went inside to negotiate with Harvey."

"Harvey came out of the store a couple of minutes ago. If this strike is over, we're celebrating." He hung up.

Harvey emerged from the group and called me toward him. I risked the value of Victoria's tea and biscuits and met him halfway.

"Did Victoria forget something?" I asked.

"No, we reached an agreement." He grinned broadly. "Strike's over." He pointed his thumb over his shoulder. "She wants you to meet her inside. Something about tacky prom dresses she didn't approve?"

I gave him a tight smile. "Great. Thanks."

I left Harvey and passed through the picketers when a fresh round of fireworks was detonated. This time they sounded closer, though the noise faded into the background, having become part of the morning soundtrack.

The accompanying screams were new.

A spear of panic shot up my spine and down to my feet. Those weren't fireworks.

They were gunshots.

I spun around. My chest tightened. Picket signs clattered to the asphalt, and several protestors did too. I ran back through the crowd and searched for the police, the shooter, or something to prove what I suspected wasn't real. But past the picket line, lying on the ground, was something I'd never wanted to see in my life.

Two men lay motionless in the parking lot. One was Harvey Monahan.

The other was Detective Loncar.

3

SHOTS FIRED

I RAN across the parking lot toward the detective's body. Someone screamed my name, but I kept going. I dropped onto my knees and grabbed Loncar's hand.

"Detective?" I said. "Come on, Detective. Open your eyes. Please. If you don't, I'll—I'll—I'll—" Paralytic fear crept through me. I couldn't think clearly and was desperate to say something to make him wake. "I'll have to find the shooter myself." For all Loncar's "Stay out of this Ms. Kidd" lectures in the past, a tiny part of me hoped the threat of my involvement would shock him back to consciousness.

He didn't respond.

I called 911. "Emergency in the parking lot outside Tradava East. Shots fired into a crowd. Two people hit. Please, hurry." I remained on the line while the dispatch officer took down my name, location, and details about the shooting. I kept my other hand gripped around Loncar's.

I let my phone drop from my ear to the ground. Loncar's eyes opened, and he stared up at the sky. He blinked a couple of times and tried to sit up.

"Don't move," I said. "You were shot."

"Who else?"

"Harvey Monahan. The union leader."

"Condition?" Loncar asked.

"The bullet went through his shoulder," said a voice behind me.

I turned and saw Eddie squatted by Harvey's body a few feet away. Eddie had taken off his cat hat and pressed it against Harvey's wound. The attractive strike leader had lost the air of confidence that had surrounded him earlier, and his dark complexion seemed to have paled. His eyes were trained on Loncar. He moved his hand to Eddie's hat and held the knit in place. Next to him, the middle-aged cheerleader stood with her hand to her mouth. Her eyes were bloodshot, and tears streamed down her cheeks. I looked back at Eddie and tipped my head toward her. He stood and turned her away from the sight of the two men.

Loncar started to move, and I put my hand on his chest and restrained him. "This is not your investigation."

Despite my level-headed instructions, the detective pushed my hand away and sat up. Everything I knew said he shouldn't move until paramedics arrived and made sure he was okay.

"My job is to protect these people."

"Right now, your job is to protect yourself." Sirens sounded in the distance. They seemed too far, like they would never arrive. I turned to Eddie. "Can you get everybody into the store?"

Eddie, who earlier had worn an expression of I'm-so-over-this was quick to nod. His eyes were wide and reflected the panic I felt.

By the time the police cars and paramedics pulled up to the scene of the shooting, the parking lot was close to empty. Clouds overhead had broken up, and soft, white puffs glided by, like wads of cotton pulled from aspirin bottles. I knew Eddie could have used help with the crowd, and I knew management in the store needed to be notified. But I couldn't bring myself to leave Loncar and Harvey. I waited between the two men until paramedics arrived and moved them onto a gurney.

A paramedic pressed an oxygen mask over Loncar's face. He pushed it away. He grabbed my wrist. "There's going to be an investigation into what happened here. I need you to leave this alone."

I kept my tone light to counter my internal shock. "Maybe the thought of me getting involved is the motivation you need to recover." My voice broke on "recover."

Loncar's hand moved from my wrist to the front of my sweater. He clutched at the bulky knit and pulled me down so my ear was next to his mouth. "This wasn't a random shooting. It was about me."

"You know who the shooter was?" I asked, surprised by what Loncar said.

"Make your statement, and then you're out." He took a labored breath. Paramedics pushed his gurney away and moved him into the back of the ambulance.

Amongst the arriving help was a dark-gray sedan with a Kojak light on the roof. The man who got out was Detective Madden, a newer addition to the Ribbon Police Department who had handled a case while Loncar was on vacation in Tahiti last December. Madden had bright-red hair, curly but tamed by a styling product, and wore a blue shirt, blue tie, and dark-blue suit. Brown wing-tipped monk straps. Navy-blue argyle socks. I focused a little too hard on the argyle to help bring me back into a place of Zen.

"Ms. Kidd, isn't it?" he asked.

"Detective Madden." Men in emergency gear flooded the scene and moved Harvey Monahan. When the doors to the second ambulance were closed, I found myself once again facing Madden's extended hand. I held mine out to shake it and noticed a transfer of blood on my palm. I balled up my fist, and Madden withdrew his hand. He pulled a white handkerchief from his inside suit jacket pocket and handed it to me.

"I understand you were the one to make the call to dispatch," he said. "Can you tell me what happened?"

I clutched the hanky. "Detective Loncar is about to retire in a week. Is he going to be okay?"

Madden turned away from me and pantomimed drinking something to a uniformed police officer. I grabbed his arm and forced him to pay attention to me. "Your colleague was shot. I think you can wait five minutes while I give my statement before getting a cup of coffee."

The uniform brought a bottle of water to Madden, who took it and held it out to me. "This is for you, Ms. Kidd. What you witnessed here today must have been a shock. Take a moment to collect your thoughts. When you're ready, I'd like you to go back to the beginning and tell me what happened."

I took the proffered water, uncapped it, and swallowed several gulps. I recapped the bottle and held it to my chest. I burst into tears. I thrust the bottle at Madden and buried my head in my hands and sobbed.

Detective Madden guided me to a bench by the front of Tradava. I sat. He sat. I took a few deep breaths and fought to get control of myself.

"How's your friend?" Detective Madden asked. I wasn't sure I heard him correctly. I cocked my head and stared at him without speaking. "The one with the baby? I believe her name was Catherine Lestes?"

Madden's change of subject was jarring, and it took me a moment to remember he was no stranger to my circle of friends.

"Catherine—Cat. She's well. She had a new year's baby. Last year. A little girl."

"She was a nice lady. I hope things turn out well for her." He pulled his glasses off, cleaned one of the lenses with the point of his blue tie, and put them back on.

"Why did you ask me about Cat? What made you think of her?"

"Ms. Kidd, you are upset over the events of this morning. I need to take your statement, but in times like these, I find it's helpful to focus on something unrelated. Something pleasant. I remembered your friend and assumed she had a healthy baby, and that seemed like a pleasant subject."

"Yes, but that doesn't change the fact that a shooter fired at a police officer in this parking lot this morning."

Madden's eyes lit up. I stared at him and considered what I'd said, what I'd remembered, and why he seemed so interested.

"What?"

"Is that your statement? That a shooter fired at a police officer?" He turned away from me and shielded his eyes while taking in the parking lot. "There was a rally of union workers in front of the store. There was already a heated scene, and as management arrived, the confrontation would have risen. It stands to reason that the shooting was accidental and the victim was random, but you're the closest thing I have to a witness."

"I am?"

"You are. And if you don't mind, I'd like to hear your statement."

Anger toward Detective Madden would accomplish nothing. My resentment toward him was born out of my fear that Detective Loncar would not recover, but if I were to help find who did this, Madden was the one I needed to trust.

"I'm working with a representative from Piccadilly Group—the new owners of Tradava—on a grand reopening. Her name is Victoria Pratt. She and I have been out here all morning."

"Doing what?"

"Sampling tea and scones." I turned to the tent. The red teapot had gotten hit by a stray bullet and lay in a pile of broken clay. The tablecloth was saturated with tea which pooled by my folder. I moved it to my handbag and flipped the tablecloth up to contain the mess. If I hadn't been off tea this morning, I was now.

"Where is Ms. Pratt now?"

"Inside the store. She and Harvey had a meeting with senior management about the union demands. Harvey came out and said Victoria wanted to see me in the store, so I headed inside."

I knew there was something wrong with my chain of events, but I kept talking while my memories were fresh.

"I heard the shots right after I got through the crowd. I was facing the store. My back was to everybody. When I turned, all I saw were people and picket signs on the ground. Nobody had a gun. If you're right about the heated scene and the potential for arguments, then Loncar wouldn't have been part of the crowd, he'd be in front of the crowd. And for someone to hit him and nobody else, it seems to me that he's right. He was the target."

"Do you know why Detective Loncar was at Tradava this morning?" Madden asked.

"No."

"What were the two of you talking about?"

"A party. His party." I pressed my lips together and stared at a loose pebble by Madden's monk strap. "Captain Valderama asked me to plan Detective Loncar's retirement party, and I approached Tradava about using the grand reopening party space to save time and money. We'll already have tables and chairs set up, and the joint press between the police force and Tradava would go a long way to help both. Loncar seemed to already know something was up. I confessed."

Madden nodded along as if it made sense. He showed neither appreciation nor disdain for my idea.

"I'm not stupid," I said, interjecting what I thought he was thinking. "I know the captain asked me as a joke— well maybe he did need somebody to plan the party, but Loncar and I haven't been best of friends since I moved back to Ribbon. Asking me to plan this party is a slap in the face of both of us. I agreed because I know I'll take it seriously. I didn't want to give anybody the opportunity to turn it into a farce."

"You're an independent person," Madden said matter-of-factly. "Whatever you plan, there's no reflection on the force."

Why were we talking about Loncar's party? Why weren't we talking about the shooting?

"Detective Loncar said he knew who the shooter was," I said. I studied Madden's face, hoping for signs that he knew too.

"When did he say that?"

"When I ran to him after the shots. I thought he was unconscious and I tried to wake him with a joke. What kind of person does that? He was shot, and I made a joke."

Madden didn't answer my question. "What did he say?"

"He said the shooter was after him, and I was to give my statement and then walk away."

"Ms. Kidd, the police force appreciates your cooperation in this matter. We will be in touch should we require anything further from you."

The ambulance drove toward the exit. The second ambulance followed closely. In under a minute, the vehicles were out of my line of vision. "Where are they taking him?" I asked.

"That is not your concern."

"But what if I want to visit him?"

"Detective Loncar will be closely monitored in private quarters." He pulled out his card and handed it to me. "Should you remember anything else, do not hesitate to call."

After the police left, the store requested all members of management make the rounds and send staff home. The store closed early. The single benefit of already being on a depressing sales trend was that staying open wouldn't have made that much of a difference.

I doubted I'd remember anything that I hadn't already told Madden. I collected my things and drove home. That's when I realized what had bothered me about my statement to Madden. Victoria had gone inside Tradava with Harvey, but Harvey was in the parking lot when the shooting happened.

Which meant either Victoria had been incredibly lucky by dawdling inside the store, or she'd known not to come out in the first place.

4

———

LATE

PERHAPS NOW IS a good time to explain why I was knee-deep in plans for a party Detective Loncar didn't want instead of manifesting a peaceful life with my new husband.

Nick Taylor and I got married in a decided-on-a-roulette-wheel-bet in Las Vegas last August. It's been eight months, and we are still in our honeymoon phase. A fact that may or may not have to do with the fact that Nick's been out of the country for the past month.

As a shoe designer, Nick spent about half of the year traveling. Recent trouble had destroyed his business, and he'd taken a year off to regroup. Two months ago, he left a multi-city tour of Asia to explore the possibilities of producing a luxury sneaker collection. This was the first time we'd been apart since being married last August, but long before then, I accepted that Nick's business required him to spend months at a time out of the country. It was the price I paid for getting free footwear. Despite knowing what I was getting into when I married him, it had been harder than expected to watch him leave.

In my attempts not to violate the no-interruptions-during-work rules we established before he left (which, may I point out, were my idea), I surrounded myself with his presence. I wore his cologne. I drove his truck. I slept on his side of the bed, although that was more of a concession to my cat Logan.

Get PoPT! says it's essential to create a world where we want to live instead of accepting an environment where we don't thrive. So while Nick is in China, I've been focusing on how to be a better person. I even ate a salad two nights ago.

But there was one thing about life with Nick that was a big question mark: children. Which possibly was the kind of thing we should have talked about before spinning that roulette wheel in Las Vegas, but I figured we'd deal with it later.

Turns out later was now. Because I was late.

Ten days late.

I would be more than happy to sit here and tell you all about Nick's possible luxury sneaker collection, but Nick doesn't want to jinx anything until after he'd found a production team.

And I could go on and on about married life with Nick (except for his disturbing habit of watching . . .

sports. Sports! I didn't even know I paid for those channels.)

But while I'm not thinking about Nick's sneaker collection or how much money I could demand back from the cable company for those sports channels I never asked for, I'm also trying not to think about how many days past thirty I can attribute to random fluctuations in my cycle.

In short, I needed a distraction.

Loncar's retirement party had fit the bill.

Loncar's shooting was going to bump that party for a problem that required far more bandwidth.

I glanced at the clock and calculated the time change to China. Nick would be asleep.

The first week that Nick spent in China was a comedy of missed phone calls and interrupted sleep schedules. After the night I fell asleep during phone sex, we agreed on a call schedule. It factored in his rigorous work demands and my not-a-morning-person needs, and we agreed we probably weren't phone-sex people. But calling Nick now, the night before his last full day at the factory, was unscheduled.

I could email him.

Except this wasn't email news.

There was no way to summarize what had happened without stressing Nick out. There was nothing Nick could do for Loncar while he was in China, and it was far better for him to focus on establishing his new business.

Nick's personal growth would demand acknowledgment of the "rescue Samantha" tendency, and when he heard this news, he'd probably charter a flight home. And since I had a newfound appreciation for empowerment and prioritizing our individual personal goals, I thought it best to let Nick finish what he started.

My self-help podcast was totally working.

I drummed my fingers on the table and considered Loncar's presence at Tradava. He wasn't in the habit of following me around. In the past, he'd made it clear he wanted me to stay away from anything involving the police. But this time, he'd invaded my turf. Why?

He knew something was going to happen.

Detective Loncar had accepted a position on the Ribbon Police Force a few years before I gave up my career in New York City and moved back to town. There was absolutely no reason our paths should have crossed. He was a homicide detective, and I'd been the designer shoe buyer for a luxury retailer. What he spent on his wardrobe in a year was what I spent on one pair of shoes.

But three years ago, I'd found the dead body of my new boss in an elevator at Tradava, and that's when we met. It had been a somewhat rocky road since then, involving counterfeiting schemes, cold cases, arsonists, and mafia, but somewhere along the line of me ingratiating myself in his investigations, I learned the crime rate in our town had steadily been on the rise. It was the reason he'd taken the job. It wasn't comforting to know our perceived idyllic town was a hotbed of criminal activity.

I approached Tradava's senior management and presented my idea. Two parties for the price of one. Giving back to the community. Celebrating a public servant. Getting positive press. They said yes. I got to work. It was the kind of juggling that could blow up in my face, but it was okay. I had a plan.

Then, strike.

Boom.

In addition to the complications that arose with the strike, there were a few other things I needed to consider.

Fact: Tradava was hurting. Sales were down. Staffing was nonexistent. Payroll was bleeding, and while we all held our breath to see what Piccadilly Group would do when they officially took over, the store was suffering.

Fact: Job security is more guaranteed when you keep yourself busy with an active workload that your new employer thinks you are the only person to handle, which was how I came up with the whole thing.

Fact: Focusing on Loncar's party would give me access to Loncar's life.

I reached for the folder of plans for Loncar's party and flipped it open. Captain Valderama would know by now what had happened, but the appropriate thing to do was to let him know the party was off. Until Loncar recovered, there was no way for me to plan a celebration.

That's when I realized the folder I'd brought home

from Tradava wasn't mine. Harvey had set one on the table for Victoria, but she refused it. When they went to the meeting, he must have picked up the wrong folder. Because when I flipped through the contents of the one I'd rescued from the spilled tea, I didn't find Eddie's design concepts or contact information for the all-female punk band or the ten best local caterers for fish and chips.

I found information on the strike. And that info might have pointed toward motive.

5

———

THIS WAS DIFFERENT

THE FIRST PAGE in the folder was a list of employees from Tradava. I ran my finger down the list and found Eddie's at the bottom, written in with a few other last-minute additions. The second page had a recap of dates, meeting times, and demands. On the third page was today's date above the heading ACTION PLAN. Below, written in handwriting that tilted forward at an almost unreadable angle, was a list.

alert the press

amass most massive rally to date (hire ringers?)

dress code

prepare statement and demands

wait until the police arrive

MAKE THEM TAKE NOTICE

These were Harvey's plans for the strike. He'd known the cops were on their way—had he been the one to tip them off and draw Loncar to the scene? But Harvey had been as much of a victim as Loncar. He'd been shot in the shoulder. Was this part of his negotiation tactic? Would he literally take one for the team?

This wasn't like the other times I'd gotten mixed up in Detective Loncar's investigations. This was different. I could make excuses for my behavior in the past: helping a friend in need, clearing my name from the list of persons of interest, and protecting my loved ones.

All along, a tiny voice in my brain had quietly stated that when I was happy, when I was satisfied, when I found what I'd been searching for all this time, my instincts to run toward chaos and danger would fade. And just like the voice that questions my second bowl of ice cream after ten p.m., I'd learned to ignore those doubts and questions and believe that someday, everything would settle down and I'd be normal.

But if that tiny voice was right, if I had everything I wanted—including a job with benefits, a steady paycheck, professional respect, and the love of a man who accepted me for me—and a shooter infiltrated that world and destroyed my inner circle, then what peace did I have? I couldn't sit by and let him or her get away with it.

I flipped through the pile on the table and found the police captain's number. He answered before the first ring ended. "Valderama."

"This is Samantha Kidd," I said. "Is there any news?"

My whole body filled with nervous energy. I walked around my dining room table just to keep in motion.

"Detective Loncar is in ICU at the Ribbon hospital," he said. "He's in a coma."

"Are they allowing visitors?"

"Right now, just family. If his condition improves, they'll relax the rules."

"Thank you," I said. I didn't mention the party. Until Loncar recovered, there were more important things to consider. "Captain, I found some notes from the union strike leader that indicated he expected the police to come to Tradava this morning. Do you know why Detective Loncar was there?"

Valderama didn't answer right away. When he did, it wasn't what I expected. "Detective Loncar is part of a task force that's investigating the rise in drug trafficking in Pennsylvania. The patterns are unusual. Like someone's moving in temporarily and then getting out before they can be caught. We're looking at businesses that could easily hide illegal activities. The strike at Tradava fit the bill. He went to check it out."

As I circled the table, my sight rested on Harvey's folder. "Did Harvey Monahan know about the task force?"

"Yes," he said. "Detective Loncar had been in touch with Mr. Monahan about the possibility that someone would use his strike as a front. Mr. Monahan was cooperating fully."

And Harvey Monahan had been shot. That didn't seem so random anymore.

I thanked Valderama and hung up. Logan jumped on the table, and I scooped him up, held him close, and set him on the floor. I refreshed his water and food. I cleaned his litter box. I emptied the dishwasher, carried out the trash, and collected the errant shoes scattered around the first floor and put them away in my bedroom closet upstairs. I changed the sheets, started a load of laundry, and bleached the grout on the tub. I felt like a robot programmed to perform mind-numbing tasks with no feeling or emotion.

The second floor of my house consisted of my (and Nick's now) bedroom and master bath, the hall bathroom, and my sister's old room, which had first become a walk-in closet and morphed into a home office. I dug out a stack of metallic white dry erase boards from the closet and carried them to the kitchen. I placed six whiteboards by the base of the dining room wall before realizing whatever notes I took, whatever I wrote and affixed to those shiny magnetic surfaces, it wouldn't be enough. I couldn't sit here in my house and try to reason why someone had opened fire on a crowd at Tradava. I had to do something. Anything.

I shrugged into a red Paddington coat and pulled on white Wellington rain boots. I added a quilted white Burberry hat, grabbed my white crossbody handbag, and drove Nick's truck to the hospital. It was fifty-five degrees.

Not particularly cold. But no matter how many layers I pulled on, I couldn't get warm.

———

THE LOBBY of ICU was filled with police officers. Men and women in uniform stood in small conversational clusters by empty chairs, holding disposable cups of coffee and talking amongst themselves. I felt their unasked questions when I entered the room.

A petite woman with a blond, mushroom-shaped poof of hair separated herself from the group and approached me. She wore a white turtleneck under a jacket made of patchworked black leather. The Dynasty-era shoulders made an unfortunate marriage to the Bon Jovi fringes that dangled from the back of the sleeves.

"Geri? I'm Bridget. Thanks for coming." She put her hand on my upper arm and tried to steer me away from the group.

"I'm not Geri," I said. "I'm Samantha. Samantha Kidd."

Her hand dropped, and two things became clear. This wasn't the first time she'd heard my name, and she wouldn't be heading up my fan club. "You shouldn't be here," she said in a low voice. "Turn around and leave."

"I want to check on Detective Loncar." I looked from her to the officers around the room. They stared back at me. It had been a long day for everyone, and the aroma indicated as much. Bitter coffee mixed with spicy after-shave and a hint of B.O.

I hadn't expected a warm reception, but this was chillier than I'd been in the car. I strode into the center of the room and addressed the officers.

"I don't care what you think of me. I know I've made some mistakes in this town, and I know there were times when you all thought I was working in opposition with you. Detective Loncar and I had an understanding."

"He understood that you were a thorn in the department's side," said a heavyset man with thick black hair and a full mustache. The name *B. Pennino* was embroidered on his black jacket above a patch that said Security.

"What I understand is that he was shot," I said. "Somebody shot a cop. Outside my place of work. I don't know who did it, and I don't know why, but I'm going to find out."

"Lady, give up the ghost," B. Pennino said. "This isn't River Heights, and you're not Nancy Drew."

"Good one, Bob," said a balding man with a nose shaped like a pickle. He and B. Pennino—Bob—knocked knuckles. A couple of others snickered.

"Yeah," said a tall man with thinning hair slicked away from his face. "Go home. We don't need your help."

Rumbles of agreement joined in. I turned to the woman in the Bon Jovi jacket, looking for some female solidarity. The men who'd been baiting me turned their attention to her too, as if curious how she would respond. Her expression was sour.

"You're not welcome here," she said.

The officers created a united front against me. I could have turned and left, but I stood my ground. The back of my neck grew prickly. My heart thumped so hard I pulled my coat closed so they couldn't see.

A man in a gray suit that closely matched the shade of his hair came out a hallway next to the vending machines. "Samantha," he said. He held out his hand. "Kirk Valderama. Nice to meet you face-to-face."

"Captain," I said. I shot a quick look at the hostile cops to get a read on their reaction. They were watching, but the energy in the room had shifted. It was one thing to intimidate me in front of their peers, but it was another to let their superior see them bully a civilian. I stood a little straighter and shook the captain's hand. "How is he?" I asked.

"Not well. The detective slipped into a coma on the way here, and there haven't been any changes. The doctors said there appears to be no permanent damage, but the longer he remains unconscious, the more unlikely it is that he'll recover."

"Are they allowing visitors?"

"You'll have to check at the desk on that."

I thanked the captain and approached the visitor check-in desk. It was about twenty feet from where the officers waited. A man in traditional blue scrubs over a white waffle-weave pullover greeted me. I kept my voice low and steady so as not to let the cops know they'd left me shaken.

"Hi," I said. "I would like to visit the man who was brought here today after the shooting at Tradava. His name is Loncar." I paused. "I don't know his first name."

"Approved visitors," the orderly said. "Are you one of them?" He tipped the end of his pen toward the cops.

I kept my eyes on him. "No. I'm a friend. I was there when the shooting happened. I was hoping—"

"You were hoping to see your friend and reassure yourself that he's going to be okay."

"Yes."

"I'm sorry, ma'am. Doctor's orders. If I could approve visitors, my lobby wouldn't look like free donut day at Dunkin'."

I pressed my lips together. It was the first thing that had brought a smile to my face since this morning. "None of them are on the visitor list?"

"There are three names on the visitor list. Peggy Loncar, Geri Loncar, and Samantha Kidd."

"Samantha Kidd?" I asked. "I'm Samantha Kidd!"

"You're Samantha Kidd?"

"Trust me. In this crowd, there is absolutely no benefit to lying about that." I pulled my wallet from my handbag and handed four forms of ID to the orderly. (It seemed prudent to be thorough.)

"Ma'am, your license and passport are enough. I don't

need your loyalty card for the pizza store or your discount card for pretzels." He handed the cards back, and when I went to take them he asked, "Little Cheesers—yes or no?"

"Definite yes." I smiled. "I'm iffy on the pretzel rods."

He grinned. He picked up a wristband that was labeled visitor and wrote on "Loncar," today's date, and a floor and room number. "Hold out your arm," he said.

I glanced at the cops. Bridget stood by a cluster of cops and made no pretense to hide that she was eavesdropping. The attention focused on me multiplied as nudges and whispers directed others to the view of me getting a visitor bracelet when they could not. Bridget scowled at me and then stormed out of the lobby.

I pretended I wasn't being watched and collected my identification from the orderly. "Third floor," he said. "Room Two B." He looked at the clock mounted above the elevator wells. "Visiting hours are over at nine."

"Thank you," I said. I turned to leave, and then, considering we'd bonded over cheese pretzels, turned back and pushed my luck. "Have Peggy or Geri been here to see him?"

"I can't share that information," the orderly said. "Sorry."

I thanked him anyway and went to the elevator wells, arrived on the third floor, and asked the nurse which way to Loncar's room. She pointed to the left and went back to her computer. I rounded the corner and was pushed out of the way to make room for a rush of medical staff who raced down the hall in the direction of a high pitched *beeeeeeep*. My pulse doubled in speed. Adrenaline made my arms feel awkward and useless. As I approached the end of the hall, I knew something was wrong.

I stood in the doorway and watched as a team of medical staff pushed an oxygen mask over Detective Loncar's face. And as I stood helplessly by, the machine that marked his heartbeat with a series of rapid beeps went steady while the spike of his pulse flatlined.

6

ONE OF THEM?

PHRASES I RECOGNIZED from *Grey's Anatomy* were called out, and the specialists in the room reacted to each other like they'd been practicing for this moment for years. The nurse who had given me directions to Loncar's room grabbed my arm and whirled me around. "Who are you?"

"That's my detective—"

She cut me off. "You need to leave. Now." She blocked my view and closed the door behind me.

I went back to the elevator but didn't get on. I couldn't leave. I was one of three people approved to see Loncar in the hospital, the other two being his wife and his daughter. And despite everything I said, I had no illusions about my relationship with the detective. Loncar wanted me to stay out of the crime wave of Ribbon, and when I ignored him, I complicated his life. So why was my name on that list? Why me and not any of his coworkers who waited in the room below? The last thing he'd said to me had been for me to stay away from this.

Who had put me on that list? Approving me meant something. I knew it did. Loncar couldn't investigate the shooting, and he wanted me to do it for him.

Don't you even say what you're thinking! I already know he couldn't have been the one to put me on that list —not if he's in a coma. But I needed to do something. And for the foreseeable future, there was nobody who could stop me.

Except maybe the shooter.

Reality check. Maybe there was another reason Loncar put me on the list?

No! I couldn't just sit around and do nothing. Not now. Not after everything.

The elevator doors opened and closed without me. Eventually, I climbed on and rode to the fourth floor, got off and wandered around the hallway in a daze. I didn't know where I was going or what I expected to find. I just knew I wasn't ready to go back downstairs and face the thin blue line.

What if it was one of them?

The thought hit me like a water balloon on a hot day. The shiver that I hadn't been able to shake since the shooting was replaced by an uncomfortable heat that prickled my armpits and climbed my neck and face. I felt sick. I clawed at the toggles on my Paddington coat and ran to the closest ladies' room. I shed my coat and pushed up my sleeves to run my arms under cold water. I was burning up. When I glanced at my reflection, my face was beet red.

I was in a hospital. I was floors away from medical professionals who could give me a once-over and reassure me that I was okay. But I knew I wasn't okay. My temperature was fluctuating between hot and cold. My stomach had been in a constant state of nausea, and I hadn't eaten pizza for days.

I knew what was happening was different than anything I'd experienced before in my life, and it didn't have to do with Loncar or the shooter or the strike or the angry police officers downstairs. It had to do with that thing I was afraid to think about.

With shaking hands, I pulled my phone out of my handbag and called Nick. Before he'd left, we agreed that the time change would make it difficult to connect while he was gone. Privately, I knew the more he was able to focus on researching factories and sourcing materials, the sooner he'd know if this new venture was viable and the sooner he could come home. There was a twelve-hour time difference between Ribbon and China, and the risk in calling him now was interrupting a business meeting.

"Hey Kidd," he answered. His voice was smooth and jovial, and he spoke as if we'd been in the middle of a conversation. "I was just thinking about you. The factory had these sneakers with a Union Jack on the side, and I pulled a pair from production for you. This marriage is the gift that keeps on giving."

It was too much. Nick calling me "Kidd" like he'd done since we met in New York. The mention of the British theme of my secret-not-secret party for Loncar. The seven thousand miles between Ribbon and China, the events of the past twenty-four hours, and the nausea that I hadn't been able to shake even after eight cups of tea. I blurted out the thing I'd tried to ignore by focusing on everything else.

"Nick, I think I'm pregnant." And then the nausea won, and I threw up in the sink.

———

I've never felt so alone in my life. The floor of the bathroom where I tossed my cookies was, coincidentally, on the floor for obstetricians. Nick stayed on the phone while I got myself (somewhat) under control, out of the bathroom, and into the closest doctor's office. Over-stuffed red chairs draped loosely with plastic lined the perimeter of the room. The walls showed exposed nails and hooks but no pictures. Three shades of near-identical pink had been swiped onto the wall in broad brush strokes and paint chips had been attached below to identify them as mauve, dusty rose, and puce. Three abandoned paint trays, three paint cans, and three rollers sat on the floor. Tilted against one of the plastic-covered chairs was a flat-screen TV playing a rerun of *Frasier.*

"Hello?" I called out.

A toilet flushed, and a woman appeared. She had wild, frizzy hair peeking out from under a plastic shower cap printed with cats. "Which one do you like?" she asked. She pointed to the swatches of color on the wall. "I like the puce, but puce? What will patients think when I tell them my walls are puce? No, I need something calming. Mauve. Have you ever noticed all of the muted pink colors have a U? Maybe it's a conspiracy." She picked up the middle roller and loaded it, rolled a W of paint onto the wall and stood back. "No, mauve just isn't as alive as puce. I'm right. Aren't I right?" She cocked her head to the other side. "Don't answer that. I know I'm right." She set the roller down. "Maybe blue would be better?"

For the first time since entering the office, the woman seemed to detach from her dilemma and notice me. I dropped my handbag and coat onto the floor and stood in the center of her lobby, unsure what I should say or do or say. Or do.

"Wow, you're not having a very good day, are you?" she said. She scooped my stuff from the floor and tossed it onto a plastic-covered sofa. "Sit. Relax. I'll get you something to drink. Coffee? Tea? Soda? Water? I've got it all. Juice? Wine? You probably want wine."

There was something familiar about her voice, but I was too freaked out to place where I'd heard it. She guided me to one of the plastic-covered chairs, and I sat. The tarp crinkled under me in a way that would make a room of fifth-grade boys laugh. "No wine," I said.

"Okay. I'll be right back." The woman disappeared for a moment and returned with a Dixie cup of water.

A faint, tinny voice repeated my name over and over until I remembered Nick was still on the phone. I held it out, and the woman took it. "Hello? This is Dr. Emma. Were you speaking to the young lady who burst into my office?" She winked at me. "I see. Yes, that does make sense. Of course. Here you go."

She handed me the phone. "Take your time. I'm going to return a few emails from the back office. Actually, maybe I should return some phone calls too. No. Emails are faster." She put her fingernail between her teeth and looked over her shoulder. "Or billing. Yes. I'll work on billing." She disappeared into the hallway, and I raised the phone to my head.

"Nick?"

"I'm here, Kidd. Are you okay?" I made an O with my mouth and inhaled sharply, and then exhaled in several short puffs. "Are you hyperventilating?"

"It's Lamaze. I watched a video on YouTube."

"How far along do you think you are?"

"I'm ten days late."

There was a pause. "Ten days. That's—not very late. Have you taken a pregnancy test?"

"I don't need to take a test, Nick. We're newlyweds.

And we've acted like newlyweds. And I cleaned the whole house and I haven't eaten pizza and I've felt ill for a week and I just threw up. I'm pretty sure that means I'm pregnant."

"Or it means you ate too much junk food and the house needed to be cleaned and there's a bug going around." He paused. "I thought it would be a good idea for me to give you some space to adjust to me moving in, but I'm all finished up here. I was going to surprise you. I can be home in a day. Okay?"

I closed my eyes, and his voice wrapped me in a cocoon of comfort. I felt a hint of the bliss I'd felt on our honeymoon when we were in Paris away from the problems of our lives. The memory of making out with him under the Eiffel Tower flashed into my brain, and a rush of heat traveled lower. My heartbeat picked up, and I became aware of what had gotten me into this predicament in the first place. "Come home, Nick," I said.

"The trip's sixteen hours long so you won't see me until tomorrow, but I'll be there as fast as I can. I'm going to need you to be calm about this. Can you do that?"

I took another sharp breath in and exhaled in three puffs. "Yes," I said. "I'll see if Emma will let me stay here a little longer."

"Is Emma a new friend? I don't think you've mentioned her before."

"She's a doctor. Is that a sign? That the first person I encountered after telling you was a doctor?"

"Where are you?"

"The Ribbon hospital."

"Samantha, why are you at the hospital? Maybe you should put Emma back on the phone."

Nick only called me Samantha when he was worried or trying to make a point. Or during those private bedroom (and sometimes living room and shower and once in the garage) moments when we—well, you get the picture. (What if it was the time in the garage?)

"I can't. She's busy with her billing. Nick—"

"Listen to me, Kidd," he continued. "I'll be there as soon as I can. This is us. You and me. I love you more than I ever thought possible."

A warm glow lit within me, and I held my breath and counted to ten while appreciating the bond I had with Nick. He knew me better than anybody, and he accepted me. He loved me. He wouldn't make me do this alone. He was coming home. He would be back in Ribbon tomorrow. I forgot about everything else except him and me and the baby we were going to have.

"I love you too," I said. "And I don't want you to cut your trip short because of me. Millions of women have already done this. I can do it too."

"Let me talk to your doctor again."

I held the phone against my sweater and called out to Emma.

"Is everything okay?" she asked. She held a stuffed rabbit in one hand and a fidget ring in the other.

"My husband would like to talk to you." I held out the phone. She handed me the stuffed rabbit and took my phone.

"Yes?" she said to Nick. "Of course. Yes. No. Absolutely. No, that's not likely. I'll tell her. Yes. Safe travels." She pressed a button on my phone and handed it back. "Your husband cares very much about you," she said.

"It took us a long time to get to where we're at, but I wouldn't trade it for anything," I said.

"I picked up on that," she said. "In fact, he did ask me to give you some advice. He wanted me to tell you to use the party you're planning to keep you busy. I agree, if you're working on a project, the best thing you can do is continue. Don't focus on what you're afraid is going to happen. Focus on what you can control."

Like a malfunctioning slide projector, images of Detective Loncar flashed into my brain. The expression on his face when he heard about the party. His demand that I keep him in the loop about everything. The shooting in front of Tradava. His body, down. The rush of medical staff in his room. The flat line on his monitor.

"I think if Nick knew the details, he'd say focusing on the party wasn't a good idea."

"Nonsense. Your husband's advice is right. Now go home and spend the rest of your evening working on your project." Her eyes cut away from mine to the swipes of color on the wall. "Maybe yellow?" she added to herself.

I stopped on Loncar's floor before leaving the hospital. The frantic energy that I'd witnessed in the detective's room earlier had given way to calm, but the door was closed, and a Do Not Disturb sign hung from the knob.

I went to the nurses' station to check on his condition and held out my wrist to show my visitor band. "I was here earlier to visit Detective Loncar. I was here when—when—" I turned and looked behind me, and then turned back. I didn't know what had happened or whether he'd pulled through.

The nurse checked notes on a clipboard and looked up at me. "Are you a relative?"

"No." The woman set the clipboard down, and her expression tightened. "But I am one of three people on the approved visitor's list," I added. She verified my identity through a phone call. When she satisfied herself, she leaned close. "Your friend had a cardiac event. It was after his daughter left."

"Geri was here?"

She nodded. She picked something up from her desk and dangled it in front of me. "She left a trail of leather fringes in her wake."

I took the black leather fringe and turned it over in my hands. There was one person on site who wore leather fringes, and it wasn't Geri Loncar.

It was Bridget, the hostile female cop from the lobby of the hospital.

7

CARL'S UNICORN

WHO WAS BRIDGET? And why had she been on Loncar's floor pretending to be his daughter? Something didn't make sense, and I was going to flip every rock in my way until I had answers.

The impulse to lie low and live a quiet, safe life vanished. Despite my rocky employment history since moving back to Ribbon, there was one thing I'd consistently done well.

I called Eddie from the car. "Yeah, mate," he answered in his Nigel voice.

I didn't bother with formalities. "I just left the hospital," I said. "Detective Loncar went into a coma. I had a meltdown, and now I'm headed home."

Eddie was quiet for a moment, and I wondered which part of what I'd said had caused his silence. "Dude, you want company?" he asked, his voice back to normal.

"Because I got a call about a vigil at Tradava, and as bad as I feel about what happened today, I wouldn't mind an excuse not to go."

"Meet me at my place in twenty minutes."

I could have driven home. I should have driven home.

I didn't drive home. I drove to Tradava.

It was dark and my day should have been winding down, but my brain was swirling with information, like dust particles floating around me in seemingly random patterns. Pieces of intel that may or may not have had anything to do with the shooting were just out of my reach.

And Eddie had said someone had organized a vigil, and I wanted to know who that someone was.

I pulled into the lot and discovered the idea wasn't unique to me. A news van was parked beyond the customer entrance, and a cluster of people stood near it. Some were holding candles. Yellow crime-scene tape marked off where the picketers had stood earlier and expanded far enough into the lot to render a third of Tradava's customer parking off-limits. In addition to the news people and the candlelight vigil participants, I counted three guards in black security uniforms.

From a distance, it should have been easy to spot Carl Collins from the *Ribbon Eagle/Times* in his trademark hat, ill-fitting seersucker suit, and Stan Smiths, but it was closing in on ten p.m., and the streetlamps that peppered the lot were far enough away from the group that I couldn't see him.

Why had I come here? Because it was ground zero. It was where the shooting had taken place. Loncar had said he knew the shooter. He said he was the target. But if he wasn't, then innocent people were still at risk.

I drove closer. Faces of the participants turned to watch me. I parked in one of the available spaces and got out. A tall, lanky man with a receding hairline and ruddy cheeks pulled away from the group and approached. "News or vigil?" he asked.

"Neither." I pointed to the store. "I work here."

"Store's closed. Probably going to be closed for some time. Might not ever reopen."

"Is that your opinion or has some official source given you a quote?"

He smiled a half smile and scratched the side of his face. Light from the nearby streetlamp made silver follicles of his beard sparkle. Instead of answering, he held out his hand. "Frank Mazurkiewicz. *Ribbon Eagle/Times.*"

"Samantha Kidd," I said.

He pointed at me, his index finger and thumb sticking out like a gun. "You're Carl's unicorn," he said. "He's been chasing you around Ribbon for years now."

"I expected to find him here tonight. Did the paper expand the crime beat?"

"Carl's on a cruise somewhere in Bermuda."

"And you're the backup crime reporter?"

"Sports." He shrugged. "I was working late on a story about local swimmers, and the editor needed someone to cover the shooting. I came here to check things out and found a vigil."

My relationship with the local newspaper was solidly tied to Carl Collins, and his absence from this investigation made it seem even wonkier. But there was an easygoing friendliness to Frank. He seemed to accept the assignment as part of his job, but not feel propelled to leverage it for bigger and better things.

"How long have you been here?" I asked.

"About an hour. I thought we'd get a background picture for the story, but people started showing up. I'm more interested in the human interest angle. You've got a family-owned business that's been here for seventy-five years, bought out by an investment company with a history of buying up retailers and breathing new life into them. You've got a unionized workforce on a picket line. And you've got a shooter who took what might have been a local story and blew it up into national news." He looked at his watch. "Seven o'clock on the west coast. Yep, by now every news station in the country has reported on what happened here today. Depending on how I write this thing, we can look like a hotbed of criminal activity or a community that pulls together in the face of crisis."

"You're going with community."

"Seems better for Ribbon," he said.

I pointed at the small crowd. "Do you know who organized this? If it were someone from Tradava, I'd think I would have been notified."

"You want to talk to the young lady in the earmuffs. Her name is Taryn." He pulled out his phone and scrolled through his notes app. "Taryn Monahan."

Monahan? That couldn't be a coincidence.

I thanked Frank and approached the vigil. As I got closer, I picked out the woman in the earmuffs and recognized her as the middle-aged cheerleader from this morning. She greeted each newcomer and handed them a thin white candle with a round disc affixed to the middle. She held her lit candle out, and they lit theirs from hers. With the expanded crowd, the glow provided what the streetlamps did not.

"You're Taryn?" I asked.

"Yes," she said. She pulled out a candle for me. I waved her off. "I'm not here for the vigil."

She stood there with a candle in each hand, one lit, one not. "You don't want a candle?" she asked.

"No. I'm not staying."

"Why not? Don't you care about what happened here today? Don't you care that someone used violence to shut down our rally?"

"You think the shooter had something to do with the union strike?"

"Of course, he did. It was probably arranged by *management.*" She said "management" like she was saying "two-month-old lettuce that's been left to rot in the refrigerator." (Not that I'd know.) "My brother was shot."

"Shouldn't you be at the hospital with him instead of here?"

Taryn pressed her lips together, and her eyes filled with tears. I remembered her standing over his body while Eddie used his cat hat to apply pressure to Harvey's wound. Taryn had seemed helpless then too. But people react to crisis differently, and paralytic shock wasn't abnormal.

"He'll be okay," I said. "He's got excellent care."

"When the press reports that employee lives were risked thanks to unfair working conditions, there's no way management can ignore the issue." She shook her head.

"I don't think you should make people think the two incidents were connected. The police have a working theory. Your brother wasn't the target."

"You were here?" She asked. She squinted her eyes. "Wait. I remember you. You were under the flag with Victoria."

"For you, it was a rally. For me, it was a day of work."

She stepped backward. "I can't believe you have the nerve to show your face here. Tonight of all nights." She turned her head to see if anybody was paying attention and raised her voice. "While my brother is battling an injury sustained while standing up for better benefits and working conditions for his peers," she called out over the heads of the crowd.

"The Ribbon hospital is a state-of-the-art teaching facility," I said in a regularly modulated voice. "They're the number one employer in the city."

"You small town people with your small town views," she said, her voice low again. "You don't know anything. Now that Harvey's practically unconscious, it's up to me to make sure the store coughs up the money they should have been paying their employees all along."

"I think you're confused about what's going on with Tradava."

"I'm confused about nothing. I talked to one member of the visual department who said he can't remember the last time he earned overtime. Those are *abhorrent* working conditions."

Taryn's raised voice held the crowd's reaction. I didn't know if it was misplaced anger over the shooting or if she'd compartmentalized her emotions and was leveraging the moment for the cause, but she successfully shifted the lens onto the lesser event from the day. People who'd quietly stood with their candles in both hands now raised them in the air and formed a crowd behind her.

"The member of the visual department you spoke to was Eddie Adams. He's their director. Do you know why he can't remember being paid overtime? Until two weeks ago, he was on salary."

Taryn's eyes narrowed, and her face squinched in anger. "Don't try to talk about things you don't know. I'm intimately aware of the background of every person who participated in our strike, and I will make sure the attention from what happened today will get us what we deserve."

She jabbed her lit candle toward me, and the flame swept the fuzzy threads of my sweater. I swatted at it before the fire caught. Taryn's candle went out. The look on her face suggested she could reignite her candle without a match. She stormed away and left me wondering if her rage was how she dealt with the tragedy, or if it indicated something worse.

8

MANAGEMENT

I BACKED away from the group and found myself in the company of Frank the sports reporter and his cameraman. "Did you hear any of that?" I asked.

"Hard not to. Is any of what Taryn said true?"

I shrugged. "I *am* management, if that's what you're asking."

"What department?"

"Corporate. I used to work in the advertising department, but when the store started having trouble, they closed advertising and gave me a temporary assignment."

Frank squinted at me. "I wondered how you managed to keep your job after that mafia situation went down in January."

"After Carl's profile on me, I ended up with a certain amount of job security."

The short version: the local paper had done a

profile on me. What should have been a feel-good puff piece that featured Tradava's upcoming collection turned out to expose facts that brought down the retailer. The store couldn't fire me without it looking like a direct response to my involvement, and since I'd almost died at gunpoint, their lawyers had probably advised them that the lesser evil was keeping me on the payroll.

It was the poetic irony of my professional life. I'd spent ten years employed by a luxury retailer, had worked my way up to senior buyer for ladies' shoes, and earned a six-figure income. I wore high fashion bought with an employee discount, lived in a glamorous apartment, and traveled to Europe four times a year.

My inappropriate flirtation with one of my designers fed my ego, and my occasional dates with the deli counter guy kept me in cold cuts. But when my parents announced they were selling the house and moving to the other side of the country, I knew the only thing I wanted was to feel like I belonged—and I didn't belong in the life I was living.

I accepted a job offer at Tradava and moved into the house where I'd grown up. It should have been simple. Local girl returns to her roots. But when the man who hired me turned up dead on my first day, I was suddenly without a job, without security, and without a future. Four years later, I was married to the designer I'd inappropriately flirted with and had iron-clad job security. My cold cut drawer was on the empty side, but for the sake of marital bliss, I paid retail for salami.

A more paranoid person might have thought the shooting was about her.

Since my background was in buying, that's what Tradava now had me do. They flexed me from department to department to oversee and approve orders. For the past month, I'd been the fashion advisor to the existing buyers in an attempt to give the store assortments a sense of continuity. Thanks to the grand reopening, we were slated for a shipment of Union Jack sweaters, Hello London! handbags, and a triple order of Jacob's Twiglets. If all went as planned, Loncar's party would serve the double purpose of giving Tradava a much needed sales bump just as Piccadilly Group was making their final decisions on staffing.

"You said you were going to write a human interest piece," I said. "Is that still your plan?"

"Do you have a different angle?"

"I might. It's too soon to tell. But can you hold off on painting anybody as a victim until I check a few things out?"

"I can't print anything about the victims until I confirm their identity and condition. Right now, everything's hush-hush."

"There might be a reason for that. What else do you know about the shooting?"

We walked to the back of the news van, and Frank

pulled open the doors. He filled two cups from a thermos and handed me one. "Hot chocolate," he said. "I'm not much of a coffee drinker."

Frank, it turned out, knew less than I did, but that didn't stop him from picking my brain to get caught up. I described the events of the morning in as much detail as I could recall but left out the conclusions I'd reached that should go to the police first.

"What about you?" I asked. "Did you pick up on anything since being here?"

Frank shook his head. "Mostly just people standing around talking. Taryn handing out candles. The cops have been staying out of the way. Two of them went to Brothers Pizza before you got here."

"The cops? Where?" I asked. He pointed to the security guards. "Those aren't cops. They're security officers. You can tell by the identification patch on the sleeve of their jacket." Sports beat or no sports beat, I was surprised Frank had made such a rookie mistake.

"They're cops moonlighting as security officers," he said. "Tradava doesn't have a lock on underpaying their employees."

I stared at the men in uniform. I hadn't paid much attention to them when I arrived, mostly because I assumed they were independent contractors hired to keep an eye on things overnight.

But the closer inspection paid off. I recognized Bob Pennino, the portly cop with the porno mustache who'd given me a hard time in the hospital lobby. He and the officers with him must have come here while I was melting down in the OBGYN wing with Dr. Emma.

I put my hand on my abdomen and closed my eyes. I was calmer than I'd been in days, and why? It was like Emma had said. I needed a project. Something to focus on instead of myself.

Frank swirled his hot chocolate a few times and then swallowed what was left. He took my empty cup, stacked it in his, and put them both inside a black plastic garbage bag behind him.

I promised Frank I'd share anything of value that I discovered, and we exchanged phone numbers. I left the van and walked back to Nick's truck.

"Well, lookie here. If it isn't public nuisance number one." Bob Pennino stood a few feet away from me. He rocked back on his feet and his security jacket opened, displaying his ample belly. "Get in your car and leave. We don't need help from the amateur sleuth society."

"Are you sure about that?" I asked. "Seems to me you have a major problem and can use all the help you can get. Isn't that what the police advocate? See something, say something?"

"Doesn't apply to you."

"What is it with you people? I'm not breaking the law, and I'm not in anybody's way. I want the same thing you want."

He grinned and narrowed his eyes, the effect making him look like a stoned Oliver Hardy. "Doubtful."

"Okay, then call Detective Madden. I have information I'd like to pass along to him."

"Call him yourself."

"Yo, Bob!" shouted one of the other security guards. "You wanna grab a beer?"

"Be right there." He turned back to me. "Mind your business, Ms. Kidd. We haven't caught the shooter yet, and I would hate for you to get caught in a follow-up display of violence." He shoved his meaty hands into his pockets and walked away.

———

EDDIE WAS WAITING on my porch swing when I got home. Logan was on the windowsill on the other side of the bay window, swatting at the back of Eddie's head.

"Hey," I said.

"Dude," he replied. Apparently Nigel was on temporary hiatus.

I unlocked the front door and led Eddie inside. The power drill was still on the dining room table, and whiteboards were scattered around by the baseboards. It felt like a year had passed since I'd dug them out of the closet to mount down here to start an investigation into who had shot Loncar, but it had been mere hours.

Eddie pulled two glasses out of the cupboard. He

uncapped a large jug of kombucha that he'd left in my refrigerator for occasions like this out and filled his glass. "You want some soda? Wine?"

Eddie was the healthiest eater I knew. If he drank kombucha, then maybe I should too. "I'll have some of that," I said.

Eddie didn't move. His eyebrows slanted in suspicion. For a few seconds, the only sound was the ticking of the kitchen clock on the wall.

"It's from my podcast," I said. "*Get PoPT!* says we should try new things."

"You're a creature of habit. Trying something new means pepperoni on your pizza."

Eddie knew me well. We'd first met in high school, though we didn't become close friends until I moved back. We were able to communicate via a verbal shorthand that occasionally included "Yo," "whoa," and the ever-present, "dude." When Nick and I spontaneously decided to marry in a Las Vegas wedding chapel last July, I Skyped Eddie in for the ceremony. But still, I couldn't figure out how to tell him that I thought I was pregnant. It was one thing telling Nick. With Eddie, it was a whole different ball of wax.

He once confronted me over my inability to confide the imperfections in my life. He claimed by not telling him what was going on, I didn't trust him to help me through my problems. As the various ways my life was going to change swirled around my brain, my stomach twisted again.

"Don't leave me hanging," I said. I held out my glass, and he filled it. I drank the contents, and it took every ounce of restraint not to make a face. "Do me a favor?" I choked out. "See if there's anything about the shooting on the news."

Eddie left the kitchen, and I chased the kombucha with three gulps of birch beer. I joined him in the living room. He scrolled to a national news channel. A woman in a sleeveless dress and long brown hair curled into sausage ringlets addressed the camera.

"A shooting in the parking lot outside of Tradava department store in Ribbon, Pennsylvania, has left a community shocked. Employees of the store gathered earlier today to take a stand over unfair business practices that were rumored to be enforced at the store, recently acquired by British private equity firm Piccadilly Group.

"Two victims were rushed to the local Ribbon hospital, where they remain in intensive care. The police have confirmed that one has reached stable condition. The other is being monitored closely. They are not releasing the names at this time. If anyone has information that can help lead to the capture of the person behind this horrible crime, please contact Detective Madden at the Ribbon Police Department." A phone number appeared on the bottom of the screen.

Eddie dropped onto the sofa. "Cop shooting. When they catch this guy, he's never going to see the light of day. If you ask me, this has nothing to do with Tradava. It's probably one of those nutjobs with a bunch of photos taped to the inside of their van."

I stared at Eddie. I hadn't talked to him since this morning, and I'd been so busy reacting that I hadn't stopped to consider that maybe the situation had been unfolding in front of my eyes.

I flipped the folder open and scanned the same paper I'd looked over last night. "This is a list of every person involved in the strike," I said. "Captain Valderama said Loncar was part of a task force to investigate pop-up drug trafficking rings. Harvey was cooperating with the investigation. Did he say anything about that to the strikers?"

"No, but he and his sister were on the need-to-know wavelength. It's not like they told us their master plan. Why?"

"It says here he had something big planned. Something that would make the police show up and the news take notice. Now he's in the hospital and Loncar's in a coma. What if this is all about Harvey? What if he was the target and Loncar was the accidental victim?"

DOUBLE AGENT

I HANDED EDDIE THE FOLDER, and he scanned the contents.

"Where did you get this?" he asked.

"Harvey brought it to Victoria this morning. It was right before they went into Tradava to negotiate. He tried to give it to her, but she didn't take it. When they went into Tradava, he must have picked up my folder instead of his."

"What was in yours?"

"Plans for Loncar's party."

"Where are they now?"

"I don't know. Does that matter?"

"I guess not." Eddie flipped through the pages from Harvey's folder. "You said he brought this to Victoria?" I nodded. "That doesn't make sense. They were negotiating against each other. Why tell her what he was planning?"

I didn't have an answer to that question either. Considering Harvey and Victoria were on opposing sides of the negotiations, his gesture didn't make sense. "Unless she's unofficially working with him to get the demands met? Maybe *she's* the double agent."

"Dude," Eddie said. "You have got to stop watching shows about the CIA."

I took the folder and flipped it open again. "Victoria and Harvey left together. Loncar showed up and asked me a bunch of questions about what I was doing. That's weird, right? He's not in the habit of hanging around the store. He certainly wasn't there for the two-for-one sale on dress shirts."

Eddie tapped the folder. "Did you tell anybody about this?"

"I told Detective Madden everything I knew, but I thought this folder was full of my plans for Loncar's party. I didn't know it wasn't mine until I brought it home."

"That's not what I mean. Management would have taken that file and used it to damage the effectiveness of the strike. You having it and not telling anybody could be viewed as you protecting Harvey's plans."

My stomach roiled. What Eddie said was all well and good—or it would have been, if not for the shooting. If I'd taken that file to the senior management of Tradava, then they would have run interference and the shooter wouldn't have had an opportunity. And I didn't want to say it, but Eddie was right.

The truth was when there was a battle between employer and employees, I sided with the support team. Regardless of my pay structure, my job was in support of the store's business. I didn't oversee anybody. I worked behind the scenes to make sure we were stocked with dark chocolate peanut clusters and three packs of cotton panties and Eagles jerseys and prom dresses.

"I need to give this folder to Detective Madden," I said. "Maybe it's important. Maybe not. It's not up to me to decide."

I fished out the card Madden left with me and called. "This is Samantha Kidd," I said when he answered. "Have you heard anything about Detective Loncar's condition?"

"No updates. If anything changes, I'll let you know."

"Detective—" I said before I lost my nerve. "I need to talk to you about what happened at Tradava earlier today. This isn't me inserting myself into your investigation. I have—I may have—a lead. I think it's best if you decide."

"Where are you calling from, Ms. Kidd?"

"I'd rather not say." Eddie held his hands up and mouthed Why Not? I pointed at the dry erase boards mounted around the walls of my kitchen, and he nodded his understanding.

"Why don't we meet at—" my mind went blank. I scanned the papers scattered on the table for help. Amidst the plans and the lists was the ad I'd seen for the band I'd been hoping to hire for Loncar's party. *The Ex-Pistols at Whiskey Mick's*. They went on stage at nine.

"Whiskey Mick's," I said. "On Penn Avenue."

Eddie's eyes widened, and I looked away. I'd just suggested meeting a cop in a whiskey bar, and if I were pregnant, then I couldn't drink! Except nobody knew I was pregnant. (I didn't even know if I was pregnant.) Which meant meeting Madden at a bar was actually a pretty good idea. It would surely undo any suspicions Eddie had after I drank the kombucha.

I shuddered at the memory.

Yes. I could get Detective Madden to drink while I had water. He'd loosen up. He'd tell me about his investigation. I could use this to learn something.

I was a natural at this informant stuff.

I finished making plans and hung up. When I turned around, Eddie was buttoning his coat. "What are you doing?" I asked.

"I'm coming with you. For backup."

"Madden is a cop. He should be a fairly safe companion."

"Have you ever been to Whiskey Mick's?"

"No. Why?"

"It's a cop bar. You're going to walk in there with Detective Madden and stick out like a sore thumb. And I've never seen you drink whiskey. You need me. You need me to make you look like you belong."

We took separate cars. Eddie had made a case for conservation, company, and convenience, but since Eddie's new apartment was less than a mile from

Whiskey Mick's, carpooling would have likely meant me sleeping on his sofa. And while I wouldn't have minded not feeling alone, I liked my bed.

I found a parking space a block away from the bar. This stretch of Penn Avenue had recently been revitalized with bars, restaurants, and galleries. It was the hot spot for social life, and local bands jumped on the event calendar. The plan was for Eddie to park at his apartment complex and walk, giving me the much needed "meeting a friend" excuse should my meeting with Madden not work out. (I didn't tell Eddie my side plan of asking the bartender to pour me a glass of iced tea in a whiskey tumbler if I slipped him a twenty. It worked in the movies.)

I opened the door and was hit with noise that pretended to be music. Raw female vocals mixed with gritty guitar chords and a pounding drum beat that pushed me back outside. I braced myself and went in. The lighting was minimal, and the dark wooden walls made the venue appear smaller than it probably was.

The bar was on the left, and beyond it were four tall cocktail tables occupied by couples. Past them, steps led down to a landing where the band played. A dartboard hung to the right of the bass player, and a group of police officers in uniform took turns throwing. Having a conversation with Madden was going to be twice as difficult with this level of noise, but more manageable with the distractions. Six of one, half a dozen of the other.

As long as Madden showed up.

The music stopped, and the general chatter of a room full of people replaced the anti-men angry female vocals. I stood between two barstools, wondering whether this had been a mistake. If Whiskey Mick's was anything like the waiting room at the hospital, this crowd could turn ugly.

A disheveled-on-purpose woman approached the bar. She wore black leather pants, a ripped white T-shirt held together with safety pins, moto boots, and an unhealthy amount of eyeliner.

"Give me a mug of something cheap," she said to the bartender, with no regard for other customers.

He leaned against the back of the bar and towel dried a glass mug. "Is that smart with Bob here?" he asked.

"Just give me the beer," she said. "I'm a customer, and I ordered a drink. Mind your business and leave mine out of it."

"Whatever you say, Iz." He set the towel down and carried the mug to the beer tap.

Iz. Izzy Smalls. I recognized her from the band's Facebook page. She was the lead singer of The Ex-Pistols.

Izzy thanked the bartender with an overdose of fake sweetness and carried her beer back toward the stage. Bob Pennino, the portly officer with the porno mustache, blocked her way. She tried to step around him, but he moved from side to side, not letting her past. The angrier she got, the bigger the smile on his face.

Until she threw her beer in his face.

Around him, other officers applauded and cheered. The wet officer grabbed a wad of napkins from a nearby table and blotted. He glared at Izzy's back as she stormed away. It seemed I wasn't the only patron to have a reason to dislike the portly cop. In need of an ally, I followed Izzy Smalls past the bar, down the steps, past the dartboard, and out the back door.

10

LOVE IS ANARCHY

By the time I reached her, Izzy had one arm out of her black leather jacket and was smoothing a nicotine patch over her bicep. She looked up when I walked out, and her angry expression relaxed. "I thought you were him."

"I think he's drying off."

She grinned. "You saw that?"

"The whole bar saw that."

"Good. Love is anarchy, man." She pulled a lollipop out of her leather jacket pocket, tore off the cellophane, and stuck it in her cheek. "Trying to quit. Nothing else works."

"You're Izzy Smalls," I said.

She squinted at me. "Do I know you?" she asked. I shook my head. "You work for the bar? I'll pay for the cleaning bill."

"I'm not out here about the spilled beer. I'm Samantha Kidd." I held out my hand.

"Samantha Kidd? You messaged me about booking The Ex-Pistols for a party at Tradava."

"I may have a job." I looked over my shoulder to the back door. "Where are the other exes? Or are they the pistols?"

"We're both. We're all ex-girlfriends who were dumped. Badly. Punk rock is good for misplaced anger." Izzy tucked the thumb of the hand not holding her lollipop into the pocket of her tight black leather pants. "Tell me about this gig."

"A British holding company bought Tradava, and we don't agree on the details of the grand reopening party."

"Tea and crumpets," Izzy said.

"Biscuits," I corrected.

"Right. I suppose you're working with that blond woman? The one who dresses like she's about to go on a fox hunt?"

"How'd you know?"

"I saw the two of you in the parking lot yesterday. I was going to introduce myself, but it didn't seem like the right time." She stuck the lollipop back into her mouth and twirled it with her hand. Her cheeks sank inward and her lips pursed, making her look like a guppy.

"You were there?" I asked. "At Tradava? Yesterday morning?"

Izzy pulled the lollipop out and pinched the stick between her thumb and forefinger. "No biggie, okay? My ex told me to show up. Said he'd give me the money he owed for our last month's rent. Should have known he was lying."

"Did you see anything?"

"Like what?" she asked in a bored voice. And then something flashed across her face, betraying her tough-girl act. "You mean the shooting, right?"

I nodded.

She shook her head. "I was gone before it happened. One sentence out of my ex's mouth and I knew he wasn't going to give me the money."

I pointed my thumb over my shoulder. "That guy was your ex?" I asked.

"Yeah. You wouldn't figure me to go for one of them, would you? Learned my lesson. They pretend to be good guys, but under the uniform, they're just a bunch of dirtbags."

I was having a hard time keeping track of where the stage presence ended and the ex-girlfriend anger began. "You left before the shooting took place. Do you remember what time it was?"

"No. I headed your way after I ditched Bob. You were drinking tea with the fox hunt woman and no offense, but we're not a tea and biscuits kind of band. I turned tail and left while the fireworks were going off."

The door to Whiskey Mick's opened, and another member of the band came out. "Yo Izzy, we're up," she said.

"About that job," Izzy said.

"It's on hold indefinitely."

Izzy bit off the remaining candy, tossed the stick onto the sidewalk, and went back inside.

I stood there in the four-car parking lot behind the bar and considered what I'd learned. Izzy Smalls had been at Tradava yesterday morning. According to her story, so had Bob Pennino.

Izzy said she'd been there when I was sampling tea with Victoria, and she'd been there when the fireworks went off. My first response after hearing the gunfire had been that it was another round of fireworks. And at least half an hour had passed between those two events.

Izzy Smalls was lying about how long she'd been at the store. She may have been lying about Bob being there too. I just didn't know why.

I SENT a quick text to Eddie to meet me out back. Minutes later, he rounded the corner. "Why are you out here? I thought you were going to cozy up with Madden."

"He's not inside. I followed Izzy Smalls after she threw a beer at her ex-boyfriend. He's a cop. Get this: she was at Tradava yesterday morning."

"Dude, she's the female Johnny Rotten. Where else is she going to find the bulk size of safety pins and plaid trousers under one roof?"

"She said she was there to meet her ex in the parking lot. Did you not hear me say he's a cop? He owes her money and told her to meet up with him so he could pay her back. She says he lied about that, but I think she's lying too. Can you keep an eye on her while I go look for Madden?"

"Sure."

Eddie went in through the back door. Instead of following him, I circled the sidewalk to the front and pretended I'd just arrived. Detective Madden was seated at the bar. It was the worst possible place for a quiet conversation where I'd optimistically hoped to ply him with booze and learn insider information. He tapped the counter next to him, and I sat down.

"Ms. Kidd," he said.

"Detective Madden," I answered. "Are there any updates on Loncar's condition?"

He shook his head. A glass with half an inch of amber liquid sat in front of him. That wasn't very much booze. Had he gotten a head start? Was he already sauced? I needed to see if his eyes were bloodshot, but I didn't know how to get a good look when we were both facing the same direction. I looked up at the mirrored backdrop behind the various booze bottles and squinted.

"I can suggest something if you'd like," he said.

"Oh. No. Why? Are you an expert on whiskey? Because if you are, I should have what you're having." Yes, this was smart. I would order whatever he was having and learn what his whiskey preferences were, and I'd order water on the side. And after he finished his drink, I'd somehow offer him mine, which would give him more than he'd probably expected, which would successfully implement part one of my plan. "Hi," I said to the bartender. I pointed at Madden's glass. "I'll take one of those," I said.

"You sure about that?" the bartender asked.

"Yes. I'm feeling adventurous."

"You want a water back?"

A water back? Back where? Did he mean water on top? As in, dilute the whiskey? "Sure," I said. "But I'd like to try it first, so on the side, please."

"A water back on the side," the bartender repeated.

"Exactly."

The bartender looked at Madden and raised his eyebrows. "Do you want to tell her?"

Madden shook his head. "Let the lady order what she wants."

I didn't know if these guys were insulting my intelligence or respecting my asserted female empowerment. (Interpreting equality signals is hard.) I smiled politely at Madden and then watched the bartender turn around, pull a miniature can of apple juice from the refrigerator, pop the top, and pour an inch into my glass. He set the glass in front of me and filled a different glass with water from the soda gun and set that next to the apple juice.

"It's on me," Madden told the bartender.

"I can't let you do that," I said.

Madden smiled. "Apple juice is free for cops. Keeps us from standing out when we patronize the place." He picked up his glass and held it toward me. I clinked it and took a sip. The cold, fruity liquid tasted so good that I gulped. "Slow down," Madden said. "Unless you want a room full of cops to think you're getting drunk on their turf."

I set the glass down and spun toward Madden. From this angle, I was able to glance over his shoulder and take in the other patrons in the room. If the reception I'd received at the hospital was any indication, then I wasn't the most welcome person. But as I scanned the interior, searching for unfriendly expressions, hostile body language, or thinly veiled, non-verbal threats, I saw none. Nobody in the bar seemed to care that I was there.

Which was both good and bad. Because this whole plan, meeting Madden, was supposed to be about trading information, getting a lead, and helping find who shot Detective Loncar. What I'd learned so far was that female punk rockers were the real deal, and cops drank apple juice off duty.

It was late, and I was tired, and this was turning out to

be a bad idea. I pulled the folder of Harvey's strike plans out of my handbag and set it on the counter.

I tapped my fingertips on the top of the folder. "This includes Harvey Monahan's plans for his strike. He gave it to Victoria Pratt, the sales executive from Piccadilly, before they went into the store on the morning of the shooting. I forgot about it until later that night when I took my files home. It's starting to seem like Harvey knew about the shooting."

"Ms. Kidd—"

"Hear me out. Maybe Harvey arranged the shooting to get national publicity for his union demands. I know that sounds extreme. That's why I'm turning this over to you to investigate." I slid the folder in front of Madden. All he had to do was take the folder, thank me for acting like a good, responsible citizen, and let me walk out of here with the warm fuzzies that come from doing the right thing.

"I'm afraid it's not that simple," Madden said. "Ms. Kidd, I appreciate you trying to help us. I'll go through this folder to see if it gives me any leads on finding the shooter. But in light of what happened to Harvey Monahan, our investigation has taken a turn. I don't think you can pin this on him."

"I know he was shot. But it was just a flesh wound, right? It could have been done to make him look like a victim and remove him from suspicion. Or it could be that he wasn't supposed to get shot and he ended up getting nicked by accident. Or maybe he underpaid the shooter who wanted to make a point. I don't think Harvey Monahan is above suspicion just because he's in a hospital bed."

"Harvey Monahan isn't in a hospital bed. He's in the morgue. Harvey Monahan died earlier tonight."

11

THE GREAT POLICE BALL IN THE SKY

"HARVEY MONAHAN IS DEAD?" I asked. "But it was a flesh wound. I thought he was faking it for publicity." This time Detective Madden had my full attention.

"The bullet that passed through his arm went into his torso. It didn't exit. When a bullet remains inside a body, it can do a lot of damage to internal tissue. By the time the doctors were able to operate, it was too late."

The air in the room felt thin. Madden's talk of Harvey's internal organs caused mine to tighten up, my stomach to clench, and my vision to blur. Eddie had sat with Harvey in the parking lot. He'd pressed his cat hat onto Harvey's wound, and when Eddie had to leave, Harvey had held the hat in place himself. If Harvey could die after seeming to be alert, then was Loncar next? Would he pull through, or was his coma simply one step on a path to the great police ball in the sky?

Whatever information I'd hoped to gain tonight paled in comparison to this news. My priorities shifted. How was I supposed to go to work now? How was I supposed to plan a party?

I could no longer accept Loncar's belief that he was the target. Harvey had died from the shooting, and no matter how dedicated he was to his cause, I doubted his negotiations involved the loss of his life.

I believed in law and order. Justice. Bad guys getting caught. And I wanted—needed—to believe that this person had left clues and could be caught.

I picked up the tumbler of apple juice, knocked it back, and slammed the empty glass on the counter. "Hit me again," I said to the bartender.

"Ms. Kidd," Madden started.

I cut him off. "I need the vitamins."

I finished the second glass of apple juice and half of my water before Madden spoke again. "We found out after the local news, but it'll be in tomorrow's paper."

"What does this do to your investigation?"

Madden shook his head. "At this point, nothing. We're still piecing together what we found at the scene, what Mr. Monahan was able to tell us before he died, and what we picked up from interviews."

"You're not confident you're going to catch who did this," I said. It wasn't a question.

"I know you understand my position well enough to know I can't confirm or deny that," he said. "But I will say

I wish we were able to get a statement from Loncar before he slipped into his coma. Cops see things differently, and he might know something."

"He did," I said. "I already told you. He said the shooter was after him. Did you look into that? Into who might have a vendetta against Detective Loncar?"

"I don't think he meant him. I think he meant the police. There's a growing rift in the community. An us-versus-them mentality. Word leaked out that you were planning his party at Tradava. It stands to reason that someone who hated cops would keep an eye on that location. People don't like that crime is on the rise, and they blame us for not doing our job."

"But why would those people do something violent? Isn't that counterproductive?"

"Shooting at the police is a surefire way to show you don't respect them."

"But they have to know you'd put all of your resources into finding who did this. Loncar was one of you." The thought, which should have been accurate, didn't fit the scene.

We were sitting in a bar filled with police officers who were shooting darts, knocking back whiskey, and listening to live music. And earlier tonight, the hospital waiting room had been crowded with police officers. All I'd seen was indifference and hostility. Aside from Madden meeting me tonight, where was the unification to catch the perpetrator of a crime against one of them?

"Why did you agree to meet me tonight?" I asked Madden. "You should be working the case. You should be out there knocking on doors."

Madden shifted his weight on his barstool. He stared at his glass and spun it around a few times before answering. "I had no plans to talk to you about the investigation tonight. I wanted to ask you about your friend."

"My friend?" I looked behind me to see if Eddie had joined us. He was on the lower level by the stage, leaning against a wall outside the restroom.

And then it hit me. Madden wanted to talk about Cat. He'd brought her up this morning. All of this, the apple juice, the conversation, and making time for me at eleven forty-five on a Tuesday was because Detective Madden wanted a date with my friend.

"Detective, if you thought you could use a meeting about finding the person who shot Detective Loncar as your own personal Tinder app, then you're not only off the mark, you wasted your time."

I took my handbag from the hook under the bar and slid off the barstool. "Thank you for the apple juice." I left.

IN TERMS OF EXIT LINES, it wasn't one of my best. The April air had cooled considerably, and a chilly breeze snapped at my face when the door closed behind me. My eyes responded by watering. I texted Eddie. *New intel. Heading home. Call me.*

He wrote back: *Roger that.*

It was after midnight, and I was exhausted. Home. Bed. Sleep. I rounded the corner to find Nick's truck, but the first thing I saw were black leather fringes. It was Bridget. Outside Whiskey Mick's. And even though we were alone on the street, there was no question that I was in enemy territory.

12

ACT OF GOD

"WHAT ARE YOU DOING HERE?" Bridget demanded. She jabbed the air between us with her finger, and the fringes on her jacket hopped about like a dancer in a Mitzi Gaynor routine.

"Meeting a friend."

Bridget scoffed. "A friend? In a cop bar? I doubt it. Nobody wants you here."

It was the second time I'd been reminded by a member of the police force that I wasn't welcome. One time, I could have understood. Two? No. Something other than my reputation was at play here, and I wanted to know what.

"What is your problem with me?" I asked. "I've done nothing to you. Nothing to your department. There is zero call for your attitude unless you're hiding something."

She was. She'd pretended to be Loncar's daughter. But before I could ask her about that, the door to the bar opened, and two men came out. A flash of fear illuminated her eyes, and then she looked away. The men rounded the corner, barely acknowledging us, and disappeared. Bridget relaxed, but moved to the opposite side of me and kept her eyes on the door.

"I've waited a long time for this, and I won't let you ruin it for me," she hissed. "You have no idea what's going on."

"Then tell me," I said. "Why did you pretend to be Loncar's daughter at the hospital?"

"How do you know about that?" Bridget squinted her eyes. She looked like she was processing what I'd said—working through whether she could trust me. I needed an ally. I reached out for her leather-and-fringe sleeve and said, "I care about Detective Loncar too."

She pushed me away and lowered her voice. "Stay out of my territory, Ms. Kidd."

I'd long ago learned it was police protocol to refer to non-police as Mr, Mrs, or Ms. I'd wasted too much energy trying to convince Loncar to call me Samantha before giving in. But this time it hadn't been said out of protocol or politeness. The vitriol in her voice said everything.

Bridget turned back toward the entrance. The door opened again, and Bob stumbled out. The scent of beer radiated off him. He'd be a good candidate for a DUI if he didn't have a get-out-of-jail-free card in the form of his badge.

"Hey, Bridget," he said. "Where's the love?"

She ignored him and went inside.

Too many things were buzzing around my head. Why did she dislike me so much? What had I done? And why pretend to be Loncar's daughter? She was pushing her way into proximity to him, which I could explain away as concern if she weren't so openly hostile toward me.

Bob leered at me. "You a badge bunny now too?"

"What's a badge bunny?"

He laughed, this time not bothering to tell me why. I felt like I was being assessed.

My phone pinged with a text from Eddie. *Band still playing. Want me to stay?*

I texted back: *abort mission.*

I practically ran to Nick's truck. I started the engine and called Eddie. "Hold on," he said while noise raged in the background. A few seconds later, the noise faded. "Okay, I can hear you now. Go."

"Harvey Monahan died earlier tonight. I thought he had a flesh wound. I thought he was behind the shooting. I thought he arranged it for publicity for the union strike. And now he's dead."

"Madden told you that?"

I nodded. "It'll be in the paper tomorrow. Madden told me because—" I dropped my head and stared at my hands. "He wants to call Cat and ask her out for coffee. He had no intention of discussing the case."

"He doesn't know you the way Loncar knows you. Like all of us know you. Remember how he was when he investigated the murder of Cat's husband?"

"I got the feeling Detective Madden is an outsider on the force, and nobody's going out of their way to make his transition any smoother."

"Maybe he's the one not doing any favors for himself."

"He was in their bar. All alone. He told me the place was filled with cops, but I didn't see one of them talk to him. It's like he's trying to meet them halfway and they're walking backward."

"Dude, Madden's ability to work and play well with others isn't your concern."

"I know."

I hung up and drove home. I realized what the feeling was that had struck me when I sat next to Madden. Familiarity. I didn't know him, and I didn't need to know him. What I knew was he was having a hard time adjusting to life in a new city. Just like I had. I blamed my hormones for my reaction inside the bar, but nobody knew about that except me, Nick and Dr. Emma at the hospital.

But the longer I went without telling Eddie, the worse I felt. Like I had this secret that I knew was going to change our friendship. I was compartmentalizing my life like a good secret agent, but it came with a price. I felt alone and desperate.

I checked the clock on the dashboard and did some time zone math. Nick would be here tomorrow. I needed to talk to Nick about Detective Loncar and Detective Madden and Harvey Monahan and then go from there.

THE NEXT MORNING, I woke, expecting morning sickness. I'd learned to tolerate the general twistiness in my tummy, but I didn't want to be lulled into a false sense of confidence. I remained in the bed for fifteen minutes, paying close attention to alien symptoms (don't tell Nick I called them that) and when I identified nothing other than a growing need to pee, I got up.

It was ten after eight. Nick would be home later tonight. Nothing would seem so scary once he was here. I just had to keep myself distracted for the next twelve hours, and then I could relax. I called Victoria and left her a message that I'd meet her under the tent. I drank two cups of coffee while waiting for her to call back. She didn't.

I searched my new Keep Calm and Carry On sweater for tags to snip. When I didn't find any, I assumed the support staff hadn't had a chance to attach them. I pulled the sweater on and paired it with black leather leggings and black moto boots. When dressed, I headed to

Tradava. I'd heard nothing about whether the store would be open or closed, so it seemed prudent to assume I still had a job.

A crowd stood in front of Tradava, but there were no picket signs, no enthusiasm, no cheerleader moves. I drove past them slowly and picked out Frank Mazurkiewicz and his *Ribbon Eagle/Times* camera crew. He looked up as I passed, and I slowed and rolled down the window.

"Frank, hi, Samantha Kidd. I was here last night?"

"Sure, I remember."

"You heard the news about Harvey, right?"

"We got the word after you left. I wrote the article in the van and made the deadline."

I should have known Frank broke the story. He'd been right here, keeping an eye on the site of the shooting. Harvey's sister Taryn had been conducting the candlelight vigil. Someone must have contacted her with the news. Where Carl was persistent about getting a story, Frank appeared to accept the bread crumbs that fell into his lap reluctantly.

"I don't imagine the union workers are planning to strike today," I said. "Have you heard anything?"

"There's a petition for Tradava to fund Harvey's memorial service, and somebody mentioned a GoFundMe campaign, but I wouldn't put much stock in either idea." He stood up straight and looked at the crowd. "If you ask me, the real victim in all this is Tradava."

"They've got Piccadilly Group signing the checks. They'll survive."

"Nope, just got word that Piccadilly found a loophole in the contracts. Mass shooting in front of a recently acquired property falls under the act of God clause. All funding was frozen."

"Piccadilly pulled out of the deal? Because of what happened here?" Frank nodded. "But if Tradava doesn't get that money, they'll be forced to file Chapter 11 and liquidate."

"Ironic, isn't it? Harvey Monahan just wanted to get better pay for half of the store, and because of what happened, everybody's going to be out of a job."

13

HUMAN RESOURCES

I LEFT Frank and drove Nick's truck around the back of Tradava. I called Victoria, and the call went into voice mail. If what Frank said were true, then Victoria would have no official reason to return my call.

The store was on a skeleton crew. I passed six cartons of Jacob's Twiglets on my way to the office and a fixture filled with folded Keep Calm and Carry On sweaters like the one I wore. The whole store was stocked with new merchandise that I'd ordered with the Piccadilly x Tradava shopping event in mind. The sweaters, like the Twiglets, were a reminder of what I'd expected to be doing right now, and the layer of dust that covered the fixture indicated how far Life had veered off course.

There was a single message waiting for me. "Call Human Resources."

This was my least favorite message. Has anything

good ever come from being called to Human Resources? Though, at this stage, I couldn't imagine how things could get worse.

I called. "Hi, this is Samantha Kidd. I got a—"

"Samantha. There's an emergency managers' meeting in HR. Come as soon as you can."

Things just got worse.

I wasted no time delaying the inevitable and arrived in HR three minutes later. John Jones, the HR manager, was waiting for me. With him was Victoria. I hadn't seen her since she left me in the parking lot to go into the store and handle negotiations with Harvey, and while her presence at Tradava made perfect sense, I was surprised to see her.

"Simontha," she said. "Please, have a seat."

Today Victoria wore a plaid blazer with suede elbow patches over an ivory silk blouse that tied at the neck. A long A-line skirt that came to mid-calf draped over the top of suede riding boots. Oxford English Professor, I thought. She reached her hand up and tucked her strawberry blond hair behind one ear, displaying a tasteful ring with a small pearl and matching pearl stud earrings.

"Am I early?" I asked.

"No," she replied. "No other managers showed up for work today."

Any other day, I would have considered it a good sign that I'd demonstrated my loyalty to the store by showing up, but it seemed the writing was on the wall.

I caught my reflection in a framed vintage Tradava ad. Dust from the store had adhered to the front of my sweater, and I swatted at it a few times as if brushing away crumbs. I sat in a stiff black leather chair with a chrome frame, and Victoria stood by the front of the reception desk.

"Simontha, I wish we were speaking under better circumstances," Victoria said. "I'd hoped for us to establish a working relationship that would see Tradava flourish under our ownership, but I'm afraid that's not to be."

"Then it's true? It sounds to me like your company never wanted to buy Tradava in the first place. Is that how you do business on the other side of the pond?"

She looked at her hands. "My employer regrets the turn of events that led us to this moment." She looked at John. "If you'll excuse me, Mr. Jones will fill you in on your severance package." She kept her eyes diverted from both mine and John's until she was out of the room.

"What is this?" I said, half to myself. "I thought we were in the clear. Piccadilly's acquisition of Tradava was in all the trade journals. It was a done deal."

"Not exactly." John leaned against the desk in front of me. He folded his hands and flicked his thumbnails against each other. The tiny movement drew attention to the one part of his anatomy that I, as his employee, shouldn't have my attention drawn to. I forced myself to look down at his shoes (black wingtip oxfords) and his socks (black with tiny teal squares). "The board of directors reviewed the contract, and there was a clause that allowed Piccadilly to back out with no repercussions."

"The act of God clause," I said. "I've heard about it. But isn't that supposed to mean hurricanes and tornadoes and flooding?"

"Yes," he said. "And mass shootings that have the possibility of leaving a negative mark on a physical property."

It felt like a weak argument. Since I'd been back in Ribbon, Tradava had been the sight of two murders. The retailer's name had been in and out of the newspapers, linked to criminal activity. "This store has been through worse," I said.

"Piccadilly wrote that off as being related to past management. They expected to take over, conduct mandatory personality tests of the remaining staff, and bring in new employees as positions opened up."

What might have sounded paranoid to someone not in the industry was standard practice. Before I'd been promoted at Bentley's, I'd been instructed to take a series of standardized tests. Everybody in senior management had. The tests determined our problem-solving skills, work ethic, and loyalty to the company. We weren't dealing in government secrets, but when you're part of a multi-billion-dollar business, your superiors want reassurance that you're part of the team.

The tests, though designed to identify strengths and

weaknesses, also called out personality flaws. People who worked well in teams and those who wanted credit for themselves. People who could see the big picture, and those who got lost in the details. People who bought into the vision of the company, and those who secretly resented their position as cogs in the machine.

Tests like that might have highlighted a person with tendencies to bring a gun to work.

"Who else knows about the testing?" I asked.

"It was common knowledge among the senior staff," John said. "The decision to reclassify the support staff was because those tests might have forced us to cut valuable employees."

I felt my forehead scrunch as I tried to understand. "You mean the reclassification of some of our managers to support staff was to protect them? They wouldn't have had to take those tests?"

"That's right," John said. "We didn't lower anyone's salary. We simply determined an hourly rate equal to their current salary. The reclassification would have benefitted people who tended toward overtime. They'd make the same amount of money for a forty-hour workweek."

I was surprised that Eddie hadn't mentioned that, but all along, he'd seemed more annoyed about having to participate in the strike than having his senior management pay bracket changed. Eddie was that rare individual who cared more about his job than anything else. With the strike temporarily paused, I wouldn't have been surprised to find him in the store assembling a Union Jack display out of colored denim.

"I'm curious. Did Harvey Monahan know about any of this? He was the strike leader and the one heading up negotiations. If he understood about the changes in pay structure, surely he would have known it was better for the staff than the way things were."

"Yes, he knew. He had a copy of the contract from Piccadilly. Harvey Monahan wasn't concerned with the salaries of our employees. The one thing he negotiated against was the standardized testing."

"Why would he care about that?"

"Samantha, before Harvey became the strike negotiator who took on Piccadilly, he was one of their employees. Something in his profile earned him immediate termination."

14

RUDE AMERICANS

My initial thought was that John Jones had no business telling me that. But then I considered what we knew. Harvey was dead. No other managers had shown up to work at Tradava. And in a matter of days, we'd all be out of work.

"Harvey told me he had an almost one hundred percent success rate with negotiations," I said. "Do you know if that's true?"

"I don't know. Piccadilly purchased retailers around the country, but companies generally don't talk about things like that."

"I got the feeling he and Victoria weren't strangers. Like maybe they've gone head-to-head before."

"It's possible. Why?"

"I'm just wondering about the shooting. Harvey and

Victoria came in to meet with you, but only Harvey came out."

"They didn't meet with me," he said. "Whatever negotiations were discussed, they happened without my knowledge."

"But that doesn't make sense. Harvey and Victoria left for a meeting, and they went inside Tradava together. Harvey came out and told me Victoria wanted me to meet her inside. I was on my way in when the shots were fired."

I thought back to the morning of the shooting. Victoria had left me alone under the flag while she and Harvey went into the store. Harvey had returned. And Victoria had vanished from the scene.

According to Harvey, the two negotiators had reached an agreeable solution. Twenty-four hours later, Harvey was dead, Victoria's company was backing out of their contract to buy Tradava, and John claimed not to know what had transpired.

I hadn't thought much about Victoria leaving me to take a meeting with Harvey, but I also hadn't realized one clause in the contract for Piccadilly Group to buy Tradava could be blown apart so easily. Victoria had been on the front lines of the buyout. She knew better than anybody what was being asked of her company and whether Ribbon would welcome a British retailer to town.

And the more I thought about it, the more I knew we wouldn't. Not the way she was looking to set things up.

She must have seen my growing frustration with the way she steamrollered every one of my suggestions.

"John, how well do you know Victoria? She must have spent time working with the Tradava executive committee. Was she happy with the collaboration? Did she think things were going well? Did she have anything to say about the strike?"

"She wasn't the most readable person, but she was decisive. I remember thinking Harvey would have his work cut out for him. It's a shame," he said quietly. "He accomplished what he set out to do, but the real victims will be the employees."

Something John said tickled the back of my brain, but I couldn't put my finger on it. "Did Victoria know about the strike when she got here? Or was it a surprise? Do people strike in England? Or is this one of those rude American things?"

"The strike alone would not have forced Piccadilly's hand. The shooting and subsequent death of the strike captain would."

I shivered. Again, I found myself wondering about Harvey. Too many questions surrounded him for me to see him as innocent.

John twisted at the waist and picked up a folder from his desk. He opened it, and his eyes moved back and forth as if reading the contents. He closed the folder and looked up. "I've been in touch with every retailer in a sixty-mile radius, and the vast majority of them were willing to fax me a list of their open jobs. Many promised priority screening to any candidates we recommend."

I'd been so focused on Harvey that I barely realized John was talking to me. I picked up the sheet of paper in front of me, the one that had "Samantha Kidd" filled out on the blank line, "bankruptcy" on the reason for termination line, and "six months severance" on the buy-out-package field. He rifled through his inbox and pulled out a manila file folder, flipped it open, and plucked out a sheet. He stared at it for a few moments, as if considering whether it was a good idea to show it to me.

"Let me be frank, Samantha. You've made a name for yourself around Ribbon, and it's not necessarily a good one. Even if I did put your name on this list, that sixty-mile radius might not be big enough for you to get away from your reputation. Nothing about this is guaranteed. Things happen around you, and more than one person on the board of directors would be happy to see you in the unemployment line."

"But you're not one of those people, are you? Because if you were, we wouldn't be having this conversation." I tapped the page with the mostly unreadable text. "You wouldn't have even told me about these opportunities. If you wanted me to be unemployed, you would have told me to sign on the dotted line, and you'd report to your superiors that you did your job." I set the paper on his desk. "I've done a lot for this store, and if they don't see it now, they'll never see it. I've done every job that's been thrown at me since the advertising department dissolved, and I haven't complained once." Slight lie, but Eddie wasn't going to tell on me. "I'm tired, John. I'm tired of working for a company that doesn't care about my dedication or want to hear my ideas." I stood up, collected my bag, and headed for the door.

"Samantha, don't leave," John said. "Have you heard any news about Detective Loncar?"

I was wary of the question. "Why would you expect me to have heard news? I'm just a regular citizen."

"Samantha, you've been involved in more than one criminal investigation since you started working here. I wouldn't expect you to try to change now."

"He's in a coma," I said. "It's been over twenty-four hours, and the doctors are starting to worry. The longer he's unconscious, the higher the odds he'll never wake up."

John grabbed a chair and turned it to face me. He sat and crossed his ankle over his knee. I put my hand on the back of the chair closest to the door but remained standing.

"Five years ago, my wife moved out," John said. "I had a hard time adjusting to being home alone, and one of the guys in my card game picked up on it. We were all neighborhood guys, and he and his wife used to invite me over—dinner, or the game, or whatever they came up with that was an excuse to let me know I wasn't alone."

The change in subject was odd but not unwelcome.

Everyone who worked for Tradava had been impacted by the shooting yesterday. John had the same amount of unresolved emotions wrapped up in the company dissolution as I did.

I lowered myself into the chair next to me and remained quiet. I suspected John had a point, and even if he didn't, for now, I was being paid to listen. But there was an intensity to the way he talked. There was more urgency in his voice now than when he'd talked about Tradava or Piccadilly or job opportunities in a sixty-mile radius.

"You were lucky to have friends like that."

He nodded. "One night, I don't know if I had too much to drink or too little rest, but I fell asleep on my buddy's sofa. I woke up in the middle of the night and felt like a jerk. I didn't want to be there when he and his wife woke up the next day. My friend's wife and I—let's just say I didn't want to be the source of more friction between the two of them. I let myself out and headed home. What I didn't know, what I couldn't have known, was that some punks had been watching my house and knew it was empty. They broke in. My ex-wife had come over earlier that night to reconcile. She was asleep in our bed while they were robbing the house. It was only a matter of time before they found her."

John's story had taken a turn into darker territory that wasn't the stuff of Hans Christian Andersen. I knew crimes like this took place in our city, but outside of what

I'd experienced myself, I'd never met anyone else with a story to tell. "What happened?" I asked gently.

"When I left my buddy's house, I tripped a silent alarm. He came downstairs to check on me, saw that I was gone, and figured out what happened." He got quiet for a moment and then continued. "My buddy was a cop. New to the city. When that alarm rang at the security company, it also rang at the police station. Dispatch sent a car before they found out it was a false alarm."

"But it wasn't a false alarm, was it?"

"The police cruiser pulled up with lights and siren on full blast. Woke up everybody in a two-block radius. Two guys ran out of my house, and my buddy caught up with them before they reached the end of the alley. When I went inside, I found gasoline cans and rags by the front door. That whole night, what could have happened, what didn't happen, it gives me nightmares."

"Why are you telling me this story?"

"Samantha, my buddy, the cop, was Detective Loncar. You're not his only friend at Tradava, but you should know that by doing his job, he's made a lot of enemies."

"Do you think the shooter was after him?" I asked.

"I think this isn't the first time someone's wanted him dead."

15

WE'RE NOT ENGLAND

JOHN CONTINUED. "When I took this job, Loncar told me to keep an eye out for you." He put his palm on top of his shiny bald head and rubbed in a circle. "I understand that you want to find answers and a person to blame. But your friend—our friend—is in the hospital. I think it would be far better for you to focus on him than worry about the fate of the store."

I left Human Resources and went to my office to pack up my desk. A ceramic double-decker bus sat by my phone. The vehicle was filled with chocolates. It was a gift from Victoria, on the first day she'd shown up at Tradava. Since then I'd seen the very same item at three different discount stores in the area. It was either a last-minute token gift, or she was mocking the stereotype of Americans who loved all things English. (My wardrobe since hearing the Piccadilly news had done little to undermine the stereotype, but that's how I roll.)

The conversation with John had left my thoughts cycling in several different directions. The information about Harvey was damning and made me wonder what else I'd find if I scratched the surface. But then there was that story about Detective Loncar. A story that could be one in a thousand that had been routine in Loncar's career. How many enemies did he have? How many criminals held a grudge against him?

Was this about Harvey, and Loncar was the accidental victim, or was this about Loncar with Harvey caught in the crossfire? How was I supposed to figure this out?

"Simontha."

I'd thought I was alone, and the surprise of Victoria's voice from the doorway caused me to jump. "I was hoping we could have a word."

"Sure," I said.

She sat in the chair opposite me. It felt odd to sit in an office, neither one of us behind a desk. She crossed her legs, and the raw edge of her suede skirt jiggled while her knee bounced.

"I guess there's no point asking how the negotiations went yesterday," I said. "I heard you and Harvey reached an agreement, but so much has happened since then."

"Yes," she said. "Well. It's a shame. The store had so much promise."

I felt my blood start to boil. "You were wrong about

us," I said. Victoria looked up from her planner and studied me. "About the store and the community. You had this idea in your head about who we were and what we'd want, but you were wrong. Ribbon may be on the small side, but people here like what Tradava sells. We're a three-generation store. Our assortments satisfy the grandmother, the mother, and the daughter. Do you know how rare that is?"

"It's not rare in England," she said.

"But we're not England. We're not going to be England. We like novelty items and fashion and sales and trends that are in this year and out next year. We like our parties to be fun. Why would people want to attend a party in the parking lot when there was no entertainment?" I hadn't realized how much I'd bottled up about the collaboration with Piccadilly, and now that it didn't matter, I couldn't shut up. I forced a shrug. "I suppose I should thank your company for pulling out of the deal."

I stood from my chair and turned my back on her. I wanted to rattle her, to shake that proper royal attitude and make her react. I wanted her to see that we weren't just chess pieces, that this wasn't just a building, that our customers weren't just wallets with people attached. I wanted her to acknowledge that by invoking the act of God clause, she was saying she believed God wanted Loncar shot and hundreds of dedicated employees to be unemployed.

Behind me, I heard a sniffle.

Slowly, I turned. Victoria was hunched over with her face pressed into a tissue. Her spine was curved too far to be normal, and her shoulders shook. Her strawberry blond hair had come untucked from her ears and hung like a curtain, shielding her face.

"Victoria?" I said.

She looked up from the tissue. Her face was flushed pinkish red, and with her mascara cried off, her eyelashes were as fair as her hair. "This is all my fault," she said between erratic breaths. She held the tissue a few inches from her face, but when her nose started to run, she seemed frozen and not capable of wiping it.

I pulled my chair closer to hers and sat back down. Had I been too hard on her? Or was she about to confess to something far worse than I'd imagined?

"What's your fault?" I asked gently.

She buried her face in the tissue again and then looked up. I extended the tissue box, and she pulled out three more and kept them in reserve. "None of this would have happened if I'd come clean with my employer."

"About what?" I pressed. Whatever it was that upset Victoria, it wasn't the three-generation thing.

"Simontha, the last time I had negotiations with Harvey, we—I—there was an indiscretion. I thought we could both be professional about it, but he leaked the information to my employer. I was suspended. Since then, Harvey has gotten everything he's asked for in strike negotiations."

"Did he pressure you to sleep with him?"

"It was consensual," she said, "It was late, we'd been discussing negotiations for hours, and he made a pass at me. I don't catch the attention of men like Harvey. I succumbed. I had no idea that he'd privately filmed us, or that he was capable of using that film to force my hand in negotiations. It was an error in judgment that I pay for daily."

"When was this?"

"Years ago. I was given this account because my colleague passed away unexpectedly and there was no one else to make the trip to the States. I had no idea I'd be negotiating with Harvey again, but this time I wasn't going to make the same mistake."

"You and Harvey went into Tradava for a meeting with John, but John said you never made it to his office. Harvey came out of the store, but you didn't. The rumor is that you reached an agreement Harvey found favorable for the union."

As we talked, Victoria's emotional outburst faded, and in its place emerged an angry, damaged woman. "He threatened me, Simontha. He said he has photos that he would use to humiliate me and undermine my position of authority."

"Harvey cared about his record," I said. "He'd say whatever he could to get results."

Victoria's fist balled up and crushed the tissue. "After what happened in the past, I'd be ruined. I agreed to reinstate all management pay grades and waive the personality tests if he would destroy the photos he took that night. But he was never going to destroy those photos, don't you see? He would never give up his leverage. For one night, Harvey made me feel like the most beautiful woman in the world, and he's treated me like a page-six girl ever since."

"What are you going to do now?" I asked.

She stood up and smoothed her hair away from her face. "I'm going home. My work here is done." She tossed the mangled tissue in the trash and left.

16

TOO. MUCH.

I WAS MORE confused than before. Had that been a confession? Victoria said she was to blame. And it was clear she felt Harvey had destroyed her life—both professional and personal.

There was no question Victoria had a motive. And while Harvey's behavior was reprehensible and I hated him on her behalf, you can't just go around shooting the people you wish you'd never slept with. Was her confession suspicious enough to take to the police? Or had that just been girl talk?

I spent the rest of the day packing my belongings into an empty box that had been used to deliver our last stash of printer paper. I didn't want to think about how my life had changed from the first time I'd stepped foot in here. I wasn't afraid of change, but this was too much change at once. Marriage. Lost job. No party. Bankruptcy. Not being able to talk to Nick for another (checks time on computer) ten hours. Favorite detective in a coma.

Too. Much.

And then there was the thing I didn't want to think about because I didn't know if I was ready. I barely had my own life together. Was I capable of caring for a baby as well?

There was a surefire way to know whether I should be thinking about it or not. I'd bought four pregnancy tests since Nick left for China, but I couldn't bring myself to use one.

I needed help.

I put my earbuds in and opened my podcast app. There were ninety-five available episodes of *Get PoPT!* and I'd listened to seventy-three of them. The remaining twenty-two talked about exercise and the importance of healthy eating, and I couldn't see how that pertained to me. I found episode twenty-two and pressed play.

"Are you feeling overwhelmed? Like you're drowning? Like every decision you make could lead to catastrophic results? I'm here to tell you they won't. You can't mess this up. Whatever you decide, it's the right decision. Now, let's do some four-seven-eights."

A wave of calm draped over me. I followed along as the host led us in a breathing technique. Inhale deeply. Hold. Exhale in a whoosh. Repeat. I felt lightheaded. That must be the result of letting go of all the pressure I'd been carrying around.

Yes. This was working. I was grounding myself. Everything would be fine.

"Breathe in, hold, and breathe out. Excellent. See how calm you feel? That's because you released yourself from punishment. Whatever it is that's causing your overwhelm is gone. Your problems will solve themselves. Whatever you decide, life will go on as it has. Breathe in, hold, breathe out."

But I didn't want life as I knew it to go on. Life as I knew it was Loncar in a coma and a shooter on the loose. It was Eddie out of work. It was Tradava on the brink of bankruptcy and a possible baby.

Or was it Loncar alive, not yet dead? Was the shooter long gone? Was there another, better job out there for Eddie? Was it better for Tradava to close their doors with their legacy as a family retailer intact than to be taken over by the Brits?

Was a baby with Nick the thing I wanted most of all?

I turned the podcast off. I couldn't allow the universe to resolve things without my input. I had to take action.

I carried my box out to Nick's truck, left it in the back, and drove to the hospital. There was one person I could talk to. One person who would listen to my deepest, darkest fears. Detective Loncar. And it's not creepy because he's in a coma. People in comas can hear us too .. . I'm pretty sure.

The waiting room was free of hostile cops, which made the check-in process go more smoothly. I took the elevator to the third floor. Geri Loncar stood outside her dad's room. She wore a white hoodie with black yoga pants, neon-orange sneakers, and a baby on her hip. The baby's tiny hand was tangled in Geri's ponytail.

When I reached Geri, she threw her free arm around me and squished me in a one-armed hug. My arms were pressed tightly against my sides, and I was unable to reciprocate even if I wanted. The baby reached out and fisted a lock of my hair, and when Geri released me from her hug, I kept my head cocked to the side to accommodate the baby.

Geri reached up and untangled the baby hand from my hair. I stepped back and smiled. "I can't believe you're here," Geri said. (The baby said "ya ya ya.")

"How is he?"

Geri shook her head, and her ponytail swung from side to side. "He's unresponsive. The doctors say he's going to wake up, but he hasn't. I spent all night researching ways to trigger a wake-up, but nothing worked."

"Did you try telling him stories about your childhood? Wake-up.com says that works."

"I admitted to smoking in his police car and blaming it on his partner. Nothing."

"Shock-awake.org says telling a parent about how you lost your virginity could do it."

"I want him to wake up, not have a heart attack."

"Did you sing to him?" I asked. She looked at me

blankly. "Comawakeupcall.com has a list of songs that triggered responses in test subjects." I tried to remember the list. "They're partial to Heavy Metal bands."

"Dad does love *Spinal Tap*," she said. "It's his favorite movie. You should do something with that for the party."

"The party," I said slowly. We stood there in the hallway outside Loncar's room, and the energy shifted from a brainstorming session to a vacuum. "There's not going to be a party. The financial backers who bought Tradava pulled out of the deal. The store is moving forward with bankruptcy filings, returning the unopened merchandise, and canceling everything on order. The HR department is handing out unemployment papers. It's over. I'm so sorry."

Geri nodded as if she understood, but I could tell she didn't believe me. Her dad was lying in a coma in a hospital bed five feet away from us, but she, like me, appeared to focus on diversion to function. "If it's any consolation, I don't think he wanted the party to begin with."

"What did you have planned?"

"Tea and biscuits," I said without enthusiasm.

"That's not really his thing."

"I know. The party I wanted to plan had Twiglets and a miniature Stonehenge and an all-girl punk rock cover band called The Ex-Pistols."

Her eyes lit up. She shifted her baby from one hip to the other. "You should tell him about that. Right now.

Pretend that's the party he's going to miss if he doesn't wake up."

"Here?" She nodded. "Now?"

She nodded again. "Go inside and talk to him. I have to find out what happened to the guard Captain Valderama promised us."

It was then that I noticed the plastic chair in the hallway. Captain Valderama wouldn't have assigned a guard unless he thought the threat against Loncar might still be realized. The empty chair indicated he might be right.

17

I LOST IT

GERI WENT TO THE NURSES' station, and I entered Loncar's room. Machines beeped at regular intervals, and a screen displayed the detective's vital signs. A saline bag hung from a metal rack next to the bed and the window at the far side of the room. I looked at the dry erase board like the ones I'd mounted in my kitchen that listed the doctor on call, the cork board filled with colorful notices about the proper way to lift a box, and the extra blanket that remained folded on the chair next to the side of the bed. I looked at everything in the room except Detective Loncar because I was afraid I'd lose it when I did.

In addition to the bed, there were two chairs and a pull-out sofa. Hospital sheets were folded and resting on the end cushion, topped with the world's tiniest pillow. I set my handbag down. I moved a chair from the wall to the side of the bed and sat down and looked at Loncar's face.

I lost it.

"You told me not to get involved," I said between erratic breaths. "You told me to stay out of it and that you knew who did this, but nobody is acting like there's an open investigation. Nobody's treating this like you would treat it. They're shooting darts and drinking apple juice and pretending everything is normal while you're lying here not doing anything. You have to wake up. You have to! Ribbon needs you. I need you. I'm pregnant! I think. And I don't know what to do!"

There was the tiniest chance that even if Loncar chose that moment to wake up, he wouldn't know what to do about that last part either. Perhaps when I finished here, I should make a side trip to Dr. Emma and inquire about a checklist.

But Loncar didn't choose that moment to wake up. He didn't wake while I told him about his party (I even threw in some references to Geri Halliwell to test him).

He didn't wake while I told him about Tradava and the memory of him tracking me down in the middle of the lingerie department on my first day.

He didn't wake when I told him John Jones had told me the story of how he saved the day by looking out for his friend and see? We're not all that different.

I was halfway through an inspired version of The Smiths' eighties classic retitled, "Detective in a Coma," when a young woman entered the room. She wore a black puffer vest over a white turtleneck and bright-blue scrubs and neon-yellow running sneakers. A backpack was strapped to her torso with a flat crossbody strap. Plastic animals hung from a silver loop on the back of the bag, and as she moved, they made little clicking noises against each other. She wore her hair in a low ponytail that hung down to her shoulder blades. The sum of the parts made her look like a Pokémon superhero.

"Knock, knock," she said.

"Oh. Hi. Sorry. I was just singing."

She nodded. "You've been Googling. We get a lot of that." She went to the machines and recorded a few readings onto an iPad and then checked the levels of the fluids dripping into Loncar's arm. "Never heard anybody go with The Smiths before," she added. There was neither judgment nor approval in her voice. To her, I was just another desperate visitor to the coma ward. "Is he your dad?"

"No, he's my detective."

"You have your own detective? Oh, you mean you're on the police force. Are you his boss?"

I glanced at Loncar's face. If something we said was going to cause a reaction, that might have done it.

Nothing.

"I'm a local resident. I've—we've—collaborated in the past." I snuck another peek at his face.

Still nothing.

"That's cool. Is that why you're here? You two were working on a case when he was shot?" She detached a plastic fluid pouch from the dangling stand and replaced it with a new one, and then moved the tube from the old one to the new as well. I watched it, mesmerized, as the fluid dripped into the tube.

"What is that?" I said, distracted from the conversation.

"Painkiller. He's not able to tell us what his pain level is, but with a gunshot wound, there's a good chance he's suffering. This is pretty mild. We don't want to risk over-medication, but if he were to wake up suddenly, we also don't want his awareness of his pain to send him back into a coma."

"Can that happen?"

"At this point, anything can happen. His vitals are stable, but it would be a whole lot better if he woke up. That's where we're at now. We want to see progress."

"What can I do?" I asked.

"You can talk to him. Tell him about the case. If he hears you, he might know something that can help you, and the desire to share that information might be what he needs." She typed a few more things into her iPad, reached over her shoulders, and in an impressive display of flexibility slipped the tablet into a pocket on her backpack.

"Do you do yoga?"

She smiled. "Talk to him. Tell him what's on your

mind. Give him a reason to wake up and tell you the one thing his subconscious feels like it has to say." She got to the doorway and turned back. "Maybe lay off songs about comas."

After she left, I considered her idea. Telling Loncar my deepest, darkest fears about my personal life hadn't created much of a reaction. And while he did know more about me than you'd expect from your normal nosy resident/homicide detective relationship, it seemed nothing I'd shared had made a difference.

I stood up and closed the door, and then took the seat by his side of the bed again. "You know this isn't fair, right?" I said. "All this time you keep telling me to stay out of your investigations and let you do your job. But this time, you can't do your job, and nobody else is doing it either. I mean, yes, Madden came out to the crime scene and took a bunch of statements, but I tried to talk to him about the investigation, and I don't think he's doing all that much to find the shooter. He's more interested in getting permission to date my friend Cat." I watched Loncar's face for a response.

Nothing.

I stood up and walked to the window. "Your daughter requested an officer be stationed outside your room, but when I got here, the chair was vacant. What if you were right and the shooter was after you? What if somebody used the whole strike situation to make you a target and hoped they could get lost in the shuffle?"

I picked up a plastic cup of now-melted ice that the previous nurse had left on the TV tray, and I stared into the water. I could say anything I wanted, but the truth was I couldn't figure this out. There were too many unknown variables and not enough leads.

There were no trees to shake, no doors to knock, no rocks to flip. Not by me, a former fashion buyer turned advertising executive turned buyer of special assortments turned party planner turned eleven-days-late new wife of a shoe-slash-sneaker designer. I needed help. I needed Loncar's help.

"I need your help," I said out loud. "Give me something. Anything. I can't do this alone." Nothing.

And then . . . was that . . . did his eyelids move?

Did his eyelids *just open?*

They did! And he blinked! His mouth opened, and his lips moved. And then he spoke.

"I thought I told you to leave this alone."

18

SET-UP

I GRABBED LONCAR'S HAND. It was cold and lifeless and dry. His arm flinched, but he didn't pull away. "I need to get the doctor. Are you in pain? She said you might wake up in pain. Do you know who you are? Do you know who I am? I'm Samantha. Kidd. We're—friends. Yes, that's why I'm here. I'm a close friend of yours. Someone you like to talk to about your cases." Should I bring up the informant thing? No. Not the right time. "Do. You. Remember. Me?" I asked slowly.

He lay still in the bed but his eyes shifted from the ceiling to mine, and I wouldn't swear on it, but it seemed that he *did* know who I was and that I maybe should have been less liberal with the friend thing. "I need to tell the staff you're awake." I let go of his hand, but he grabbed my wrist before I got out of reach and held it firmly enough that I couldn't get away.

"The strike was a set-up," he said in a barely audible voice. He closed his eyes, and that was it.

"No! You can't go back into a coma! Help!" I cried out. I pressed all the buttons on the cord that lay next to his bed. A green light lit on the wall behind him, and seconds later the door opened, and a team of medical staff came in.

I was escorted out.

It's one thing to recognize your power and take control, but it's an entirely different level of frustration when you find yourself in a situation you can't change. (*Get PoPT!* is surprisingly mute on that.) Loncar was the one person I needed to talk to and I couldn't. I used every ounce of positive thinking that I could conjure to believe he would wake up. And he had—just not long enough for me to tell him what I knew and find out what I should do.

I was looking at this whole thing all wrong. It was selfish for me to think Loncar would wake up and give me direction. He never told me what to do in the past, so why would he start now? And if I'd learned anything from *Get PoPT!*, it was that we need to never give up on what it is we want to accomplish. We need to believe, then achieve.

Actually, that wasn't half bad. Maybe when this was all over, I'd reach out to the *Get PoPT!* team and see if they wanted to use it.

Focus, Samantha.

I went to the waiting room and spotted a cluster of

cops by the vending machines. I stayed on the elevator and rode back up, this time to the fourth floor, and retraced my steps from the other night to the safe space of Dr. Emma's office.

In the brightly lit hallway, I noticed things I hadn't the last time I was here. Unlike the linoleum floor of Loncar's part of the hospital, this floor was freshly carpeted. A deep claret shade with small gray and white ziggles through it gave off a playful vibe. Doors along the hallway were painted red. Brushed chrome doorknobs, nameplates, and chair rail coordinated the design effect. ICU was sterile, but up here, I felt like I'd entered a medical building for an upscale clientele.

I used the ladies' room and then entered Dr. Emma's office. During business hours, the waiting room was busy with visibly pregnant women and toddlers (and expertly painted walls, I might add. Dr. Emma had settled on a soft shade of powder blue. If OBGYN didn't work out for her, she might consider a sideline in decorating). I went to the window and waited for the receptionist to finish her phone call.

"Hi. I'm Samantha Kidd. I don't have an appointment, but I was wondering if I could see the doctor."

The woman glanced at my tummy and then back at my face. "Is this an emergency?"

"No, but there have been some changes since the last time I saw her, and I thought it best to keep her filled in. This is all new to me, and—"

"Of course. I understand completely. Kidd, you said? Samantha? The doctor is behind schedule. Have a seat. I'll see if I can fit you in."

I sat as far away from the kids as I could and pulled out my phone. It was five thirty. Nick's flight was due to land any minute. I switched on the ringer and stared at the screen. My phone rang. The receptionist shook her head and pointed to the door. I stood and ran out and answered and dropped the phone on the hallway carpet in the process.

"Nick! I'm here! Hold on. They kicked me out of the doctor's office." I picked up the phone and pressed it against my head. "Hi," I said. "I'm here. And you're here. You're here? In Philadelphia? Not China?"

"Kidd, why are you back at the doctor's office? Has something happened?"

I'd waited too long to confide in Nick, and now there was too much to tell him over the phone. I took a couple of breaths for good measure but kept the Lamaze breathing out of it. The door to the doctor's office opened, and a woman with two kids exited. I peeked inside and saw empty chairs.

And while I listened to Nick's voice, I knew that I was going to be okay. "Hurry home. I missed you. I'll tell you everything when we're together."

We said goodbye. I reentered the doctor's office. It was approaching six, and I doubted they were going to extend their hours just for me. I waited at the front desk while the receptionist finished with a phone call. Her handbag, a black suede bucket bulging with personal items, sat on the desk on top of a blue scarf with sequins sewn into the crochet.

"Hi," I said. "I know you're going home soon, so maybe it would be better for me to see Dr. Emma another time?"

"Emma?" repeated the receptionist. "Who's Emma?"

This time I felt my face contort into confusion to match hers. "Emma. The doctor who works in this office. I talked to her the other night."

"We don't keep night hours."

The receptionist slid the glass partition closed and made a phone call. The glass muffled her voice, but I could still understand her. "This is Riley from Dr. Oplinger's office. There's a patient in our waiting room who said she was here last night. Yes, that's right. Yes, I'll tell her." She hung up and slid the glass open. "Have a seat, Ms. Kidd. Someone will be with you in a moment."

"But you said Dr. Emma didn't work here," I said.

"I said we don't keep night hours," she said. "Which means you're lying. And I'm sure building security would be interested in finding out why."

19

NAME DROPPING

I was starting to think the Ribbon hospital was cursed. "Excuse me one moment," I said. I pulled out my phone and called Nick back. "Nick? Remember the other night when I called you from the doctor's office? That really happened, right?"

"It was morning for me, but yes. Why?"

"I'm in the very same office, and they're telling me there's no Dr. Emma. You spoke to her too, remember? What did she tell you?"

"Kidd, let me talk to the receptionist."

I held out my phone. "My husband would like to talk to you."

Riley took the phone. "Hello? Oh, hello, Mr. Taylor." Her cheeks flushed, and she snuck a look back at me. "I didn't realize. No—oh. Yes. Oh, okay, that does make sense. But then—oh. Okay. Yes, that makes sense too. Okay. Thank you." She handed the phone back to me. "I didn't realize you were married to Nick Taylor," she said in awe.

"Does that matter?"

"Nick Taylor the shoe designer, right? *Footwear News's* most eligible bachelor?"

"Yes, that's him."

She moved her handbag from the desk to the counter. She held it open so I could peer inside. Nestled on top of a sparkly sweater and folded jeans was a pair of shoes from one of Nick's previous collections. "I bought them on eBay. It's my first pair of designer shoes."

Okay. Okay! We were finally speaking the same language!

"Riley, I was here, and I did talk to a woman who told me her name was Emma. The furniture was draped in plastic, and she was trying to decide what color to paint the walls. You don't know who I'm talking about?"

Riley's face lit up like a spelling bee contestant who remembers where to put the Y in "rhythm." "The life coach!" she said.

"Life coach?"

"Yes. I get it now. Emma made arrangements to use our lobby to see patients until the renovations are finished on her office. It was all very hush-hush, and Doctor Oplinger told us we wouldn't see or hear from her. I forgot all about that." She tipped her head and gave me a knowing smile. "I knew you were faking being pregnant."

"But I'm not faking," I said. "I threw up and cleaned my house and haven't had pizza for a week."

"Have you taken a pregnancy test?" she asked. I shook my head. "You're already here. Let me prep the test, and you can be sure before you drive home."

I froze. Riley was right. I didn't know anything. I thought I knew, but was this like the rest of my life? When I thought I knew something and charged ahead before I was sure?

Arguably the easiest thing on my to-do list should have been peeing on a stick. But I'd been carting those pregnancy tests around with me everywhere I went, and they were still in the bag.

Because I didn't want to be alone when I found out.

Either way.

"Nick's on his way home from China, and I'd rather do this with him. I'm sure you understand."

"I understand completely, and if you are pregnant, call me. I'll get you the next available appointment." She squeezed my hand. "And tomorrow, when I get in to work, I'll find out how you can reach Emma to set up a proper appointment. Although if you're married to Nick Taylor, your life must be perfect. Why you need a life coach is beyond me."

Bolstered by Riley's boost of confidence, I went back

to Loncar's floor. The door to his room was open. The bed was empty. My stomach lurched, and my positive thinking went AWOL. The toilet flushed, the bathroom opened, and I was face-to-face with Loncar in a hospital gown.

I covered my eyes with my hands. "I'll leave. I'll leave and come back and pretend this never happened."

"Turn around while I get into bed and then sit," he commanded.

I did a one-eighty and waited.

"Okay."

I turned back. Loncar was in the hospital bed. The sheets and blanket were pulled up to his waist, and even though I knew his non-athletic build usually strained the buttons on his dress shirts, I couldn't help noticing he looked smaller and more fragile than usual.

"You didn't listen to me," he said.

I looked down at my hands. Did I ever listen? I felt like I'd let Loncar down, and I couldn't find the nerve to tell him. The machines beeped in the background. I waited for him to say something. He didn't. I'm an impatient sort who doesn't do well with prolonged silences. (Loncar knows this.) I cracked.

"I didn't stay out of it. I tried," I said. Loncar remained silent. I looked away and then, realizing how guilty that made me appear, looked back. "I didn't try hard. But I work at Tradava, so I had to return to the scene of the crime to go to my job. And I'm one of three people on your hospital visitor list, so *somebody* knew I'd try to come here to visit you, and they made sure I could. But ask Detective Madden. I did what you always want me to do. I cooperated with the police. I can't help it if he isn't doing his job."

"Madden's a good cop."

"He wants to date my friend."

Loncar raised his eyebrows. "Which friend?"

"Cat Lestes. He investigated the murder of her husband while you were in Tahiti."

"Where was this?"

"Whiskey Mick's."

"Madden asked you to meet him at a cop bar?"

"No, Whiskey Mick's was my idea. I was scoping out a band for—" An image of The Ex-Pistols flashed into my head, and I bit my lip. "The why doesn't matter."

Loncar scowled. He picked up his cup and handed it to me. "Get me fresh water."

"I don't think they want you drinking water. I think they want you sucking on ice."

"Get me fresh water."

"Fine. I'll get you fresh water." I filled Loncar's cup and handed it to him. "Why do you care who suggested the bar?"

Loncar finished the water and set the cup down. "Madden must be thinking the same thing I am. If somebody on the force leaked information that led the shooter to Tradava, then that person might be on the inside.

You're no stranger to the police force, Ms. Kidd. You have a reputation. Some cops think you're a nuisance."

I would have argued the point on principle, but I'd recently experienced overwhelming evidence to the contrary. "Is that why Madden ordered me an apple juice?"

Loncar smiled. "The next time you see Madden, give him a break. He did you a favor. Besides, what if Madden makes your friend happy and you're standing in their way? Madden had to start over when he relocated here. Ms. Lestes is working on her own chapter two. It's not like you to interfere with people looking to move on."

Loncar wasn't talking about Cat and Madden. He was talking about himself. There'd been a time when he wanted to reconcile with his wife, but maybe that time had passed, and didn't he deserve a second chance too?

Peggy Loncar hadn't returned any of my calls about the party. As far as I knew, she hadn't used her visitor privileges to check on her ex-husband either. She'd moved on. Loncar could spend his spare time miserable if he wanted. He could throw in the towel on love, or he could question every decision he'd made that had led him to that moment when his life changed unexpectedly and the rug was pulled out from under his orthopedic shoes. And he'd never get answers. He'd never know if there was one thing that soured his wife on their marriage because there wasn't. There was never one thing.

Couples didn't break up because one person left the dishes in the sink on a random Tuesday in May. They broke up because at least one of them had a clear view of the day-in/day-out monotony of their joint life and reached a point where they couldn't take it anymore. The catalyst could be anything: an unexpected email from a forgotten high school relationship, a sudden inheritance that makes a different life possible, or a life-threating wake-up call in the form of a scary health diagnosis. The result was one person verbalizing their unhappiness and saying they wanted out. And in most cases, when one person was unhappy, so was the other, whether they admitted it or not.

Peggy Loncar hadn't done anything to the detective when she asked for a divorce. She'd done something *for* him. She'd given him a chance to find his own brand of happiness with his future. Maybe she didn't see it that way, and maybe he didn't either, but I did. And if I could see that, then I could see his point about Madden.

"I hate it when you're right," I said.

"Now you know how I feel when you solve my cases."

I smiled. "About that. You told me not to get involved in this, and I tried not to, but I can't help it. I was there. I saw things you didn't and I know things you don't."

"Like what?"

"When you were shot, you said it was about you. I don't know if anybody told you, but Harvey Monahan, the union captain, died from internal injuries."

"He was shot in the shoulder."

"The bullet passed through his shoulder and lodged in his torso and never came out. Madden said when a bullet is left in the body it can do a lot of damage. You think you were the target, but that would mean Harvey was an innocent victim."

"What's your take?" Loncar asked.

I leaned back and considered the question, barely registering how out of character it was for him to ask. "I don't think this was about you. It doesn't fit. You think someone had it out for the cops, but nobody else acts like that's the case. Harvey was at Tradava every day since the strike started. If someone were out to get him, they'd know where to find him."

"Why do you think someone was out to get Harvey?" Loncar asked.

"Well, there's Tradava and Piccadilly Group. The financiers pulled out of the deal to buy Tradava because of Harvey's death, and we're talking about hundreds of millions of dollars that Piccadilly should have had zero chance to get back after their offer was accepted."

"Business."

I nodded. "I'm not saying that's what happened, but I'm going through the possibilities."

"Any other theories?"

I took a breath to answer and then stopped myself. This had to be a trap. Contrary to the white lie I'd told the

Pokémon doctor, Loncar and I didn't sit around discussing cases.

I narrowed my eyes. "What's happening here? Why are you talking about this with me?"

Loncar turned and looked out the window. "My daughter put three people on the visitor list, and not one of them is a cop. The message is clear. Get better so I can retire. I don't want to retire. I've got nothing to look forward to except for a party I don't want. If this is my last case, I'm going to solve it."

"And me?"

"I need access. My daughter won't do it, and my ex-wife hasn't been here once."

"How do you know? You've been in a coma."

"Ms. Kidd."

"Oh, right, you're a cop. You have informants." I looked away. Real ones, apparently.

I sat up a little straighter. "Do you want me to go through the suspects? I have whiteboards at home. I could bring them here. We could set up a war room while you recover, except no, somebody might see. How about I give you the rundown?"

"Ms. Kidd," Loncar said. "I need you to do something for me."

"What?" I felt a seismic shift between us. Loncar was giving me a job!

"That party you're planning—I need you to use that."

My hopes deflated. "You just said you didn't want a party."

"I don't, but nobody has to know that. I need you to use the party as an excuse to get into my house."

"Why?"

"Because I need you to find out where my wife was the morning of the shooting."

20

DRUGS ARE WHACK

"You suspect your wife?" I asked.

"Right now, I suspect everybody."

"That's the way I work. You're usually more discerning with your suspects."

"Maybe it's the drugs."

"Yeah, drugs are whack."

The lines and planes of Loncar's weathered face were more pronounced than usual, and I wondered about the toll of lying in a hospital bed recovering. He had lived his life in search of something. Whatever the caseload, whatever the crime, he was driven to detect what happened and who did it. And here he was, the center of a crime he couldn't solve. It had to be making him crazy.

"Captain Valderama told me about the task force. He said the department has been keeping an eye on various ports of entry, and the union strike fit the profile. What does any of that have to do with your ex-wife?"

Loncar didn't respond. I sat there, silent, waiting for him to crack like I did when the tables were turned. The vital signs monitor beeped in the background, and the longer we sat in silence, the harder staying quiet became. He was very good at this.

I finally broke the silence. "Harvey left a folder of information on the table where I was working. Remember when you tried to look in the folder, and I stopped you? I found out later that folder wasn't mine. It was Harvey's plans. One of the items was to wait for the police."

"He knew we were coming?" It was a question asked in a manner that didn't require an answer. Whatever he knew, he hadn't known that. "He knew we were coming," he said again, though this time it was a statement. He'd worked through what that meant. Unfortunately, I was still in the dark.

"What does that mean?"

"It means it was a trap."

"A trap implies that someone or something is being caught. There were too many uncontrollable variables that morning to successfully set a trap."

I paused and remembered my conversation with Izzy Smalls. She'd admitted to being there, and she'd implicated Bob Pennino too. Who else had been there?

Loncar adjusted his position and then spun his hand in a circle toward him. "Give me the players."

"Aside from the strikers, there were a lot of people at Tradava the morning of the shooting. Harvey's sister, Taryn, was part of the strike."

"Who else?"

"Izzy Smalls. She's in a band that I—um, yes, she was there to meet up with her ex, a cop named Bob? Do you know him?"

Loncar nodded. "Keep going."

"It was a parking lot outside of a major retailer. There were customers and employees, and without pulling the parking lot surveillance footage, there's no way to know how many people were there." I paused. "Do you want me to pull the parking lot surveillance footage?" I asked, half hoping he'd say yes and tell me how to do it.

"Is that it?"

I guessed that was a no. I turned away and thought back to what had happened. "Victoria and I were sampling tea until she went inside with Harvey—"

"Who's Victoria?"

"Victoria Pratt. Sales executive from Piccadilly Group. She and Harvey were negotiating the strike settlement."

"She wasn't with you when the shooting took place?"

"No. Victoria and Harvey left me in the parking lot. Harvey came out and said they reached an agreement, and seconds later, the shooting happened."

"Have you talked to Ms. Pratt since then?"

"Yes. She and Harvey have a history, and it isn't particularly nice. He's been blackmailing her to get results for the union."

"How did you find this out?"

"She told me," I said.

"She told you." He didn't say it as a question, but I sensed his hint of disbelief.

"We bonded over tea."

"I thought you drank coffee."

"People change."

Loncar sat up. "Here's what I need you to do." He put his hands over his face and rubbed at his forehead as if he were trying to smooth out decades of wrinkles. When he dropped his hands, he looked more miserable than I'd ever seen him before (and now his forehead was red).

"Can I count on you?" he asked.

"I'm not going to break into your house unless you give me more intel."

"Ms. Kidd," Loncar said. "There is nothing illegal about what I'm asking you to do. I will give you my keys. Tell Peggy you want some personal items from my office. She won't give you a hard time. She's been on me to clear out that room for months. Once you're in, get to the kitchen and check the planner on the table under the phone. Can you do that?"

Maybe. "Absolutely."

"Contact every person who knows me and tell them the party is on."

"But I just told you there is no party."

"Don't worry about that. Worry about getting the word out. Whoever's behind this used you. They used me. I'm going out on a limb here, but I don't think that's going to sit well with either one of us."

He had a point.

———

I DROVE HOME. Logan stood inside the front door, meowing a welcome home/pay me attention wail. I scooped him up against my Keep Calm and Carry On sweater. He angled his head to rub against my chin. I scratched his ears and stood still, appreciating the complete peace of mind that is tangible when I'm holding my cat. Outside, a car screeched to a stop in front of the driveway. I turned my head and saw Nick get out of a black sedan and wrangle two suitcases from the trunk. Moments later, he burst through the door.

"Kidd," he said. He dropped the suitcases and pulled me into a hug. Logan, who didn't know the details of Nick's sudden return, let out a fresh wail at being squished. Nick loosened his arms, and the now-angry ball of black fur jumped down, onto the chair then the floor and ran into the kitchen. Nick pulled me close again, and I turned my head and laid it across his chest. The emotions I'd tried to keep at bay returned, and there was no stopping them. Nick's heart thumped, either from the short jog from the car service to the front door or the possibility that I might become responsible for raising his unborn child.

Gently, I pushed Nick away. "There's another reason I've been visiting the hospital," I said. "Detective Loncar was shot. In the parking lot outside Tradava. He's been in a coma for two days, but he woke up," I said.

Nick didn't say anything. He kept his arms around me, loosely, and studied my tear-streaked face. I searched his eyes for signs that hinted toward his reaction.

He put his finger under my chin and raised my face to look at his. "He's going to be okay," he said. "Detective Loncar is a tough cop. He's resilient. He'll recover."

"He looked so small," I said. "Loncar has always been this big guy with a gruff exterior. Even after I got to know him a little, I thought he was invincible. Like old shoe leather."

"He's a person. Just like you and me."

"He could have died," I said. A fresh wave of tears filled my eyes.

"But he didn't," Nick countered. I pressed my cheek into his suit jacket, and he rested his chin on my head. We stood like that for a long, intimate moment. I didn't want to talk. I didn't want to cry. I didn't want to eat. I just wanted to be.

"What if I'm pregnant?" I finally asked. "What if we have a baby and it doesn't change anything and I put myself in danger? What if bad guys get me and you have to be a single dad?"

"Shhhhh," Nick said.

"But it could happen," I said. I pulled away from Nick and studied his face. "Even if I stay out of trouble, it could. That bullet could have hit me instead of Loncar."

Nick dropped his arms and led me to the sofa. We both sat. "Did you take a pregnancy test?" he asked softly.

"I wanted us to take it together." Considering what was involved in taking the test, that didn't sound right. "I mean I didn't want to find out by myself."

"I'm here now. And I think you should know—*we* should know—before either one of us lets any more 'what ifs' into the conversation."

"What if the stick turns pink and I help Loncar anyway? Are you going to divorce me?" My breathing became erratic, and hiccups kicked in. "Because I don't think I can"—hic— "but your company—and Tradava"—hic— "and China—and Eddie—and Cat and Madden—" hic.

"Kidd, hey, shhhhh, hey, come here." He pulled me close, kissed my forehead, and held me tight. "Whatever we find out, it's going to be okay. But we need to know." He loosened his arms. "This is between us. Not Loncar or my company or Tradava or China or Eddie or Cat or Madden."

"Cat *and* Madden," I corrected.

Nick leaned closer. His lips brushed against mine,

softly, gently. There was a sharp intake of breath, and then his lips pressed into mine—longer this time. My heartbeat raced, and I put my hands on his biceps and kissed back. When we pulled apart, he rested his forehead against mine and spoke in a quiet, gravelly voice. "No matter what color that stick turns, it's you and me."

"And Loncar?"

"I like to think there will be times in our relationship when Loncar won't be present."

"That's not what I meant."

He smiled. "Detective Loncar is my friend too. If he needs help, he's going to get two for the price of one."

———

I PEED ON THE STICK. We waited for the response together. And then, we knew. I wasn't ready to tell anybody yet, but we knew.

You'll find out soon enough.

21

A PROPER WELCOME HOME

NICK DESERVED A PROPER WELCOME HOME, and to be honest, the more I thought about that time in the garage, the more I wanted a repeat performance. I'd even cleared a spot on the workbench.

When we were done (that garage was becoming my favorite room in the house), we negotiated dinner (Me: how about fish and chips? I haven't tried Yelp #9. Nick: this isn't going to be like the mac and cheese in Vegas, is it? Me: On second thought, maybe we should order cheesesteaks.) I set the table while Nick lugged his suit-cases upstairs and took a post-sixteen-hours-on-a-plane shower. The food arrived, and we tabled conversation in favor of eating.

"I never thought about sneakers before," he said when we finished. "Sneakers. Leather and rubber. So simple. But they're a whole different world. Nothing like the designer shoe market. The product coming out of these factories is amazing. Once we worked out the language barrier, there was no stopping us."

"Was that a problem?"

He chuckled. "Things got weird on the third day when they started holding up samples and saying 'Samantha?' The translator finally told me they thought it was a new word for something I liked because whenever I said it, I smiled."

"You called me Samantha? You usually call me Kidd."

"I call you Samantha lots of times. When you're—and when we're—" He glanced at the door to the garage.

I felt myself blush. "But I like when you call me Kidd too."

"Which do you prefer?"

"Well, that time in the spare bedroom, you called me Kidd," I said, "but that time in the laundry room you called me Samantha. And then there was the time you called me Mrs. Taylor . . ."

"That was the night we got married."

"You seemed to like that one."

"That's because Mrs. Taylor has never gotten involved with the criminal element."

I leaned back in my chair. "Does it bother you that I didn't change my name? Because I don't think I can stop being Samantha Kidd."

"I came to terms with that before I proposed." He smiled warmly. "Kidd, face it. I know you better than anybody else. And what I don't know, I want to know." He retrieved a shoebox from the carryon suitcase he'd left by the door. He handed the box to me. "Tell me what you think," he said.

The sneakers were white leather with Union Jacks stitched onto the side in white glitter tweed. Raw edges to the fabric gave the style an edgy feel. The center of the flag started by the instep and folded over the laces, velcroing into place to complete the flag. They had a hidden wedge, which made them less unisex than if they'd been designed for sports. They were the perfect sneaker for walking from the car to the pizza store for takeout.

There was totally a market for that.

"I love them," I said. I pulled my black moto boot off and wiggled my toes. Nick propped my foot on his knee. He removed the stuffing from the sample and eased it onto my foot like Prince Charming.

"How does it fit?"

"Like a glass slipper."

The laces were white, and by the toe two small metal charms dangled: "Nick's" and "Kicks."

"You seem happy about this," I said. "Excited."

"I am. I'm ready for something new. I'm not walking away from designer shoes forever, just for now. Is that okay with you?"

I reached for his hand and squeezed. "You and me," I said.

I SPENT the rest of the night filling Nick in on the situation with Loncar. Aside from a couple of quick drive-by conversations with Eddie, I hadn't realized just how much I'd been holding in myself. It felt good to talk about everything, and it felt even better not to be judged.

"Let's see if I have this straight," Nick said. "Harvey Monahan was the union leader. He showed up at Tradava and organized a strike. Did he work for Tradava? Do I know him?"

"Harvey showed up after Piccadilly put in the bid on Tradava. He's led strikes in the last four stores that Piccadilly acquired. He used to work for them, but after Piccadilly instituted standardized testing, he was fired."

"Piccadilly Group. You said they backed out of the deal to buy Tradava after the shooting."

"Right. Does that mean something? They made an offer to buy the chain of stores. It was a good faith offer, and to the rest of the world, it was a done deal. And then there was a shooting at Tradava, which got them off the hook for their investment." I wrote *Piccadilly Group* on one of the whiteboards and underneath wrote: *motive— act of god clause*

"Kidd, it's a stretch to think a company like Piccadilly Group, who has a history of buying struggling retail chains, would orchestrate a public shooting to get out of a business deal."

I capped my marker and leaned against the dining room table. "I know. But Piccadilly has millions of dollars at stake. I don't want to ignore the possibility that money was a motive."

Equally unlikely possibilities filled the other boards: *Harvey Monahan: attention for union gone wrong, Victoria Pratt: HM blackmail* and *Cop hater: random target.* (That was my least favorite theory. I wasn't willing to accept the pointlessness of our task if the shooting were random.)

"What are you thinking?" Nick asked.

"The day of the shooting, Loncar told me this was about him."

"I think it's normal, if you're shot, to think someone was shooting at you."

"No, I mean he got hit and went down in the parking lot at Tradava. I ran over to him. He told me to stay out of the investigation."

"No surprise there. When it comes to your involvement in police matters, Loncar plays like a broken record."

"He said it wasn't random. It was about him. And when I was at the hospital earlier today, Loncar told me to use the party as an excuse to get into his house and find out where his wife was the morning of the shooting."

I uncapped the marker and wrote *Peggy Loncar* on the whiteboard.

The request bothered me more than I cared to admit. In the years that I'd known Detective Loncar, I'd learned bits and pieces about his life. I'd also developed an appreciation for his dedication to the job. But this request of his felt less about police work and more personal.

He couldn't honestly believe his ex-wife had anything to do with the shooting. He was using me to spy on her.

There are few things you are less predisposed to do in your first year of marriage than help a divorced husband dig up dirt on his ex-wife.

"Peggy Loncar has nothing to do with the shooting at Tradava. It's a bogus job. Just like Tradava gave me. It's to keep me from doing more damage. Get me out of the way," I said.

"Are you going to do it?"

"I'll go to his house and snoop like he wants, but that can wait until tomorrow." I stood up. "Are you jet-lagged?"

"I slept on the plane. My sleep's going to be wonky for the foreseeable future."

"Then grab your keys. We're going to Whiskey Mick's."

"Why?"

I waved my hands by the whiteboards. "This has to do with the cops, and if Loncar won't tell me what's going on, I'll find out myself."

22

BADGE BUNNY

WHISKEY MICK'S was less crowded than it had been last night. The noise level was low. The Ex-Pistols tuned their instruments by the stage, and tonight there were more couples than cops. Having Nick by my side kept me from feeling self-conscious, but I already knew this wasn't destined to become my regular hangout. It took a few seconds for my eyes to adjust to the dim amber lighting, but when I did, I saw the person I wanted to see.

Detective Madden nursed a glass of apple juice at the end of the bar.

"Follow my lead," I said to Nick.

I strode toward Madden and took the stool next to him. "Two of what he's having," I said to the bartender.

"Samantha—" Nick said.

I held up my hand. "Trust me."

The bartender turned his back and filled two glasses.

He set one in front of Nick and one in front of me. I lifted the glass and took a sip.

This was not apple juice!

I set the glass down, coughed, and then glared at Madden. "You're not supposed to drink on duty," I said.

"I'm off duty. You shouldn't have come here."

"Why? Because this is a cop bar and I don't belong? You're sitting alone which suggests you aren't here for the company."

"And you brought a date which suggests you're not here for the company either." Madden lifted his glass and drank, seeming to savor the taste. Could it be he liked whiskey?

I swiveled toward Nick and took his hand, then rotated back toward Madden. "Detective, this is my husband, Nick Taylor. I don't know if you had a chance to meet him last December when you worked that case involving my friend."

Madden looked from me to Nick and back to me. They shook hands. I slid my glass of whiskey toward Madden and shrugged, and then signaled to the bartender. "Can I get a water back?"

"Back of what? You don't have a drink."

Nick stifled a laugh. I elbowed him. "A glass of water, please."

"Coming right up."

I waited until the bartender went to get a clean glass, and I turned to Madden. "Detective Loncar was on a task force to investigate drug trafficking in Ribbon."

"Ms. Kidd—or is it Mrs. Taylor?"

I glanced at Nick, and his eyes darkened. "Call me Samantha."

"Samantha, you already know I can't tell you about Loncar's investigation."

"But you know about it, right? Because he told me you're a good cop. And you're here, every night, and nobody on the force talks to you. Which tells me you're not here for the camaraderie. You're watching someone."

Madden lifted his glass and downed it. He pushed the empty glass toward the bartender but made no move to position my drink in front of him.

If he thought the silent treatment would make me go away, then he was a fool. "What's a badge bunny?"

The question caught him off guard. "A woman who likes cops. Gets turned on by the uniform. Hangs around where cops hang around."

"Like here," I said.

"You could say that."

"The last time we were here, there was a woman named Bridget. She wears a leather jacket with big shoulder pads and black fringe down the sleeves. A couple of cops told me she was a badge bunny."

Madden set his glass down and pulled his glasses off. He used the tail of his green necktie to buff the lenses and then put the frames back on. "I'm not one to engage in gossip about my coworkers, Ms. Kidd. What Bridget does with her personal time is up to her."

I leaned forward. "Bridget was at the hospital the day Loncar was admitted. She's been openly hostile toward me, along with a room full of police."

"She was hostile to a room of police officers?"

"No, they were hostile too. Two days later, Bridget tried to pass herself off as Loncar's daughter to get into his room—a room that was supposed to be guarded by a member of the force who coincidentally was on a break." I searched Madden's face for signs that something I said meant something to him in the grand scheme of the investigation and not just in the Samantha-doesn't-play-well-with-others category. Nothing. "Loncar told me you're a good cop. He told me you did me a favor by meeting me here the other night."

I thought my speech would have some sort of impact on Madden, but it didn't. I slowly climbed off my stool and made eye contact with Nick. He came with me tonight because I said it was important, and after spending almost twenty-four hours on a plane, I was pretty sure sitting on an uncomfortable barstool in a cop bar wasn't on the shortlist of places he wanted to be. But he was. Because I asked.

I put my hands on either side of Nick's face, leaned in, and kissed him. Everybody deserved a chance to be this happy.

I opened my wallet, pulled out a soon-to-be-collector's-item business card from Tradava, and wrote a phone number on the back. I gave it to Madden. "That's Cat's cell number. She hasn't decided if she's leaving Ribbon for good, so if you plan to live here, you should call her sooner rather than later."

He took the card and tucked it in his wallet. "Last night you said you didn't want me calling your friend. What changed?"

I turned to Nick. "Can you give me a minute?"

"Sure."

I waited until Nick was a few feet away before answering. "Everything changed. I used to be afraid of Loncar, and now I'm afraid he's going to die. I had a good job and the company filed bankruptcy." I paused, knowing there was one more change I had to say out loud. "I thought I was pregnant, but I'm not."

I said it. I said it out loud to someone who didn't know me well enough to know if the fact was significant.

"Does that make you sad?"

"I don't know. I didn't stop to think about what I wanted, and now I can't stop thinking about what I don't have. But I lost my job and Nick's starting a new company, and that's more change. Do you want me to continue?"

"There's more?"

"This whole city has changed. I moved here to live where I grew up, but it's barely the town I remember. Fegley's, Arners, Seafood Shanty, Bowl-O-Rama, they're all gone."

"I don't know what that means."

"It means things change, but we don't have to be sad about it. I don't know if you and Cat will get along, but I have no right to stand in your way. You were nice to her. Even if you did treat her like a murder suspect, you weren't mean about it. Call her. I think she'd like that."

"Thank you," he said.

I glanced around for Nick. "I'm going to use the ladies' room. Will you tell Nick I'll be right back?"

"Sure."

I felt like a weight had lifted, the same way I felt when I confessed bad behavior to my parents in my teen years. I'd verbalized thoughts that had been swirling around inside me. I still didn't know want I wanted, but that didn't seem like the worst thing in the world anymore.

I made my way past the stage. Izzy Smalls was in the middle of a rough cover of "Love Hurts." I entered a small bathroom with two stalls, both in use. I stood by the sinks and waited until one of the doors swung open. Bridget glared at me.

Tonight, she wore a tight black shirt with a cut-out that displayed a Y of cleavage caused, most likely, by an unnecessary push-up bra. Her fringed black leather jacket hung open, framing her chest. It looked like the slot of a coin machine, and I had a hard time looking away.

"I thought I told you to stay away from me," she said.

"I need to go to the bathroom."

"Duh, you're *in* the bathroom." She pushed up the sleeves of her jacket and elbowed me out of the way. She turned the spigot on high. Water spit out. I stepped back and bumped into the door of the second stall.

"What is your problem with me?" I asked Bridget.

"You know what my problem is. Don't act like such a goody two-shoes. I don't like you hanging around my scene. I don't like you hanging around my cop. You're not good for him, and I am, and it's just a matter of time until you're out of the picture. Got it?"

Was Bridget interested in Detective Madden?

The toilet flushed, and the stall opened. It was the drummer for The Ex-Pistols. Bridget stepped back so the woman could wash her hands. The drummer left, and it was down to Bridget and me, and I realized why women go to the bathroom in groups.

Bridget stuck her hands under the stream of water and flung her wet hands in my face. Droplets clung to my eyelashes. "Go. Away." She grabbed the door handle and stormed out.

"Hey," I called to her back. She ignored me. The door started to close on me, and I used my foot as a doorstop. "Hey!" The crowd quieted. I felt the stare of more than one of the patrons, but instead of giving them my attention, I focused it all on Bridget. She turned back around. "He can do whatever he wants," I said. "And trust me, he can do better than you." Someone whistled low. A ripple of response fluttered through the bar. I returned to the bathroom and into the stall. There was no toilet paper.

I left the stall and washed my hands anyway, and then went back to Nick and Madden at the bar. Nick stood, and I put my hand on his sleeve. I turned to Madden. "It seems the favor you did by talking to me at this bar may have backfired. Bridget has set her sights on you, and she's under the impression that I'm in her way."

Madden's eyebrows knitted together. "Bridget isn't interested in me," he said.

"She just confronted me in the bathroom and made it clear she thinks I'm her competition. I haven't spoken to anybody else here with any regularity."

Madden looked past me, into the far reaches of Whiskey Mick's and then back at me. "Bridget is interested in one cop. All those questions about badge bunnies . . . you really don't know?"

"Know what?"

"Bridget does like cops." He held up his index finger. "One cop. When I first moved to Ribbon, I was told to steer clear of her, and I did. But it's common knowledge that she was sleeping with Detective Loncar. She's the reason he's getting divorced."

23

AN AFFAIR TO REMEMBER

DETECTIVE LONCAR HAD an affair with Bridget? The woman who posed as his daughter to get into his hospital room? The woman who the other cops called a badge bunny? The woman who flushed all the toilet paper so I'd be forced to hold it or drip dry?

Speaking of which, I wasn't going to be able to hold it forever. I shifted from foot to foot. "Are you sure about that?" I asked Detective Madden.

"As I've said, Ms. Kidd, I don't pay attention to gossip around the precinct. Loncar's wife had divorce papers served to him at work. It seemed in poor taste to me, but I don't know their history. If he cheated on her with Bridget, then I understand her choice of making a point in front of the division."

The bathroom situation was growing increasingly urgent, so I thanked Madden and pulled Nick out of the bar. "Drive home as fast as you can," I said. "I *really* have to pee."

———

ONCE I WAS minus two gallons of liquid, I was able to think. Nick was upstairs in the shower, and I'd turned down his invitation to join him to sit in the kitchen and stare at the whiteboards. I'd learned something significant tonight. Something I never expected. Something that connected back, not to the strike, or the store, but to Loncar himself.

If it was true.

A crazy coworker once led me to hide out at a motel near the police station. That's when I found out Loncar's wife kicked him out of the house. Their daughter was pregnant, and neither she nor her mother had allowed him to visit with her. The story had gone a long way in making me rethink what I knew about the crotchety man in the marine buzz cut and ill-fitting suits, and through a couple of our conversations, I started to see how hard his job was (which you think would strengthen the argument for citizens like me who wanted to "help.")

Several months later, Loncar had taken a vacation in Tahiti. I'd hoped that he and his wife had worked things out, but his wife hadn't joined him. He'd confided in me that when he got back, she wanted to talk reconciliation.

But what if he'd had a fling while they were separated? What were the rules in a situation like that? Would she understand? Or was it like Ross and Rachel being on a break?

A new picture emerged, one I wouldn't have considered in a million years. What if Detective Loncar *had* cheated on his wife while they were married? What if she found out *after* she told him to move back in? What if the other woman had been a cop? It would stand to reason that she'd be mad at the entire precinct. It explained why no members of the police force were on the approved visitor list and why she would have his divorce papers served in front of his colleagues, either to humiliate him or to let everybody know she knew the truth.

Was Peggy Loncar that sort of woman? And if she hadn't been before, was she now?

I knew one person I could ask. Well, technically I knew two, but asking Loncar about his sex life definitely crossed a line.

———

THE TIME CHANGE between China and Ribbon kept Nick from sleeping through the night, a fact I discovered in the morning when I went downstairs and found him staring at the whiteboards in the kitchen. "I made crepes," he said. "They're good with blueberry butter."

I paused. "I don't have blueberry butter."

"You had blueberries." He paused. "Why do you have blueberries?"

"I was going to bake you a pie."

Nick eyed the blueberry pie in the middle of the table. "What's that?"

"A pie."

"Where did it come from?"

"The bakery."

"Isn't that your pie dish?"

I averted my eyes. "I'm better at presentation."

"Lucky for you, I work well with refrigerator items that are on their way out, so I made the butter too." He spooned a blob of blueberry butter onto a crepe and then flipped the crepe closed and handed the plate to me.

I swallowed a forkful. Nick cooking for me was an indulgence I could get used to, but it also aimed a spotlight on my cooking inadequacies. According to a recent podcast of *Get PoPT!,* learning to do something we felt ill-equipped to do was merely a matter of applying the principles of positive thinking.

Did ordering take-out count as manifesting dinner?

"Kidd," Nick said. "They're crepes. They're not supposed to make you feel bad about your culinary skills."

"Who said I felt bad about my culinary skills?" That didn't sound defensive at all. "I mean, I feel a little bad about my culinary skills."

"Come here," he said. He scooted his chair away from

the table. I got up and sat on his lap, and he wrapped his arms around me from behind and nuzzled my neck. "Talk to me about this investigation," he said. "Let me help."

"I talked you through it last night before we went to Whiskey Mick's."

"And then you talked to Madden, and you found out new facts, and when I came home and showered and went to bed, you stayed down here and stared at the walls."

I turned sideways and draped my arm around his neck. "How do you know that? How'd you know what I was thinking about the crepes? Do you know me that well already?" I leaned away from him as a new fear struck me. "Are you going to get bored with me?"

"I doubt you'll ever be boring." He pulled me close, brushed my hair to the side past my shoulder, and kissed my neck. "Now, tell me what all this means."

I stared at the whiteboards. I'd covered Piccadilly Group, Harvey, Victoria, the union, and the possibilities of a whacko who had chosen his victims at random. The only thing I hadn't covered was Loncar's original suspicion that the shooting was about him. For the first time since the shooting, I had information that made me think maybe Loncar was right.

"Loncar's wife sent divorce papers to the precinct. That tells me she wanted to humiliate him. The most obvious reason for her to act that way was if he cheated on her."

"I thought he said she wanted him to retire?"

"That's how I remember it. He made it sound like Peggy didn't like being married to a cop."

"So she kicks him out. Seven months later he takes a vacation in Tahiti, and when he gets back, she wants to reconcile."

"Aaaaaand, sometime after that she served him with divorce papers." I jumped up, and Nick winced. "What?"

"Bony butt."

"I'll take that as a compliment." I grabbed the marker and used the side of my hand to wipe off the notes on the whacko whiteboard.

"Hey!" Nick said.

I whirled around. "You do not seriously believe this was a random whacko. If you did, you wouldn't have been staring at these whiteboards for the past four hours."

"How do you know how long I've been down here?"

"You're not the quietest crepe maker." I turned back to the whiteboard and wrote *Peggy Loncar.*

"You don't believe his wife would hire a shooter, do you? It makes no sense. She's divorcing him. He signed the papers. Their marriage is over."

"That's just it, don't you see? She wanted him to retire. Now he's retiring, and she won't speak to him. Why? This is what she wanted. Unless there's some reason it's not."

Loncar had wanted me to get into his house. He

hadn't said why, but he'd had a reason. And now, thinking about the inconsistencies in Peggy Loncar's behavior toward him, I had my reasons for wanting to go there too.

I couldn't just show up. Even with Loncar's permission, it was too suspicious. I needed a person on the inside, someone to invite me over and make my presence seem like the most normal thing in the world.

Before Nick could respond, I grabbed the phone and called Geri. "It's Samantha Kidd."

"Samantha," she said slowly. "It's eight o'clock."

"Did I wake you?"

"No, I've been up for most of the night. What's up?"

"I was hoping we could get together today to talk about some last-minute details for the party. I have the box of your dad's things that you loaned me, but maybe I could borrow some of his personal items to set up a display?"

"You're still working on the party? I heard it was canceled."

"Who told you that?"

"My mother." Geri got quiet. "She hated the idea from the beginning. I guess she's getting what she wanted all along."

24

———

COVER STORY

THERE WAS no reason in the world Peggy Loncar should know if her ex-husband's party was on or not, and I had a feeling learning who told her would be a very good idea. "Geri, can we meet up for coffee? I want to ask you a couple of questions."

"I'm sorry," she said. "The baby was up all night, and I'm whipped. I just dropped her off at my mom's house, and I am desperate to get some sleep. Do you understand?"

Of course, I understood. I understood that thanks to a crying baby, I had an opportunity to cut out the middleman and find out what I needed to know while Geri slept. Who was going to tell on me? The baby?

"Get some sleep. We'll chat later." I hung up and headed for the stairs.

"Where are you going?" Nick asked.

"I'm getting dressed." I stopped by the bottom of the steps. "What's the appropriate outfit for stealing files while confronting an angry ex-wife with questionable motives?"

Arriving at the house once occupied by the Loncar family unit was a joint effort. In the box of items that Geri had loaned me, I found an old Christmas card still in the envelope. The address matched the one in the yellow pages in my kitchen drawer (thanks, Mom and Dad, for not throwing things out before I bought the house!). Siri gave me directions. Nick drove.

We parked in front of a red brick Colonial with black shutters and cream-colored trim. An attached garage sat off to the left of the house, leaving the driveway clear for Nick's truck. "Wow," I said.

"Wow," Nick echoed. "This is where Loncar lives?"

"Not anymore."

We got out of the truck. I'd gone for classy and upscale and avoided any clothes with the word "London." A red cotton blazer over an ivory jewel-neck sweater with a navy intarsia crown, ivory skirt, ivory crocheted tights, and gray over-the-knee boots. I draped a red scarf with an ivory windowpane pattern loosely around my neck and carried a navy-blue handbag.

"You know the cover story, right?" I asked Nick. "We're here on behalf of Tradava. We need a few more details for the party. We tried to call but probably have a wrong number or an incorrect email address. Showing up in person was our last resort."

"What's your name?" Nick asked.

I stared at him while trying to compute. "Samantha," I said slowly.

"Don't you think Peggy has heard of you? Don't you think maybe she'll put two and two together and slam the door in your face?" He had a point.

"What's my name?" I asked.

"Follow my lead," he said.

We reached the front door, and I rang the bell. The door opened quickly enough to let me know we'd been spotted from the driveway. A woman with short, fluffy gray and blond highlighted hair faced us. She had a baby on her hip and an apron that said "I Wine A Lot" on top of a stretchy scoop-neck T-shirt and mom jeans.

"May I help you?" she asked.

"Are you Mrs. Loncar?" Before she could answer, Nick proceeded. "We're Mr. and Mrs. Taylor. We're helping coordinate the retirement party for your husband, and our contact at Tradava asked us to stop by to pick up a few of his items. Someone should have called ahead about it. You did get the message, didn't you?"

She turned and looked at the staircase and then back at us. "The phone rang earlier, but my daughter was here, so I let the answering service get it. I haven't had a chance to check the messages. What did you need?"

What did we need? I had no idea. I turned to Nick,

who raised both eyebrows. I widened my eyes. He pressed his lips together and turned back to Peggy.

"I'm afraid we don't know what we're supposed to pick up," Nick admitted. "We were told to get some items from his office. Personal things. Collectibles, awards, you know, the sort of things we could use to set up a display showcasing his achievements?"

Hey, that was good! I turned back to Nick to show my appreciation and realized I was about to blow the lid off classy and upscale with my enthusiasm.

Peggy turned to look at the stairs again, appearing to think, and then turned back. "This isn't a great time—"

"We don't mean to intrude," I interrupted. "Does he have an office or a study? If you haven't had a chance to pull anything for us, we could take a look. It might be easier since we'll get what we need now and won't have to interrupt you again."

She shifted the baby to the other hip and started a slow bounce. The baby grabbed for her dangly earring, and Peggy tipped her head just in time to keep the wriggly girl from making contact. "Could you hold her for a minute?" she asked me. "She's been trying to grab my earrings all morning, and if she gets one, I'm pretty sure I'll never wear pierced earrings again." She held out the baby toward me.

I froze.

"I'll take her," Nick said. He took the baby and held her up in the air. "Hello there," he said. She giggled. He tossed her in the air a few inches and then caught her and cradled her in his arm. "You're a cutie," he said. He touched her nose, and she produced a bubble of spit.

"Thank you," Peggy said. She was earringless. I'd been so mesmerized by the sight of Nick with that baby girl that I'd lost track of Peggy. She could have disposed of evidence right under my nose.

The baby was a wild card I hadn't properly factored into the equation. This could get tricky.

Peggy took the baby from Nick. "The office is down the hall, second door on the left. Take whatever you want." In the background, a toilet flushed. Peggy turned and looked over her shoulder and then back at us. "I'm going to put the princess to bed. You'll be quick, won't you?"

"Of course," Nick said.

Neither one of us spoke until we were in Loncar's office. I shut the door behind me, and Nick opened it back up. "She'll think it's suspicious if the door is closed," he said.

"She's supposed to be overjoyed that the party was canceled, but she didn't think it was suspicious that we showed up and asked if we could take her ex-husband's stuff. Isn't *that* suspicious? She didn't mention they were getting divorced or that he doesn't live here. She just went along with what we asked. You probably could have asked to leave with the baby and she would have said okay."

"I think she may have drawn the line at the baby."

We didn't have a lot of time to find whatever it was we were hoping to find, so I glanced about the room and made a quick assessment. "We have to leave here with something," I whispered. "Grab his football trophies and his framed detective certificate. What's that black thing over there—a Kevlar vest? Take that. Look for a scrapbook." I turned toward the door and raised my voice. "I don't feel so well."

"You're sick?" Nick asked.

"I need to use the bathroom," I whispered.

"From the crepes?"

I lowered my voice to a whisper again. "The bathroom is upstairs, and somebody flushed the toilet while we were talking to Peggy. There's somebody else in the house, and I want to know who." Nick nodded. "Peggy?" I called out softly.

She appeared at the top of the stairs. She'd taken off her I Wine A Lot apron and fluffed her highlighted hair. "Are you done already?" she asked.

I stood in the doorway so Nick could hear. "I'm not feeling very well. Could I use your restroom?"

"Of course. Right here," she said. She knocked on an open door. I ascended the stairs and passed her while she stood in the hallway. "Did you find anything?"

"My husband is making a few selections. You wouldn't happen to have a box we could use to carry them out to the car?"

"I'll see what I have in the garage."

I went into the bathroom, and the door, which had warped, didn't close properly. I pulled the door open and tried to shut it again. No luck. The third time I opened it, Peggy stood on the other side. "You have to slam it to get it closed. You go in. I'll get it." I stepped back, and she grabbed the doorknob and gave it a strong push. The door clicked into place with a *bam!*

There was no way I could sneak out and snoop. There was no way for me to get out, period. And even if I did, how would I know which way to go? What did I expect to find? A teething ring and empty jars of baby food in the recycling bin?

This house was a grandmother's dream, not a coverup for hiring a shooter to take out her ex. There wasn't going to be anything suspicious here.

Except the toilet seat was up.

I wasn't in the mood for commode forensics, but the position of the toilet seat suggested that a man had been the last person to use it. And I'd heard the toilet flush while in the study with Nick. Those two facts made me curious.

I picked up a chipped plastic cup that sat next to the toothbrush and pressed it against the door with my ear. There were voices.

Two voices. One male and one female, and the male wasn't Nick. When I couldn't make out what they said by the door, I climbed onto the vanity and listened by the vent. No luck. I climbed back down and spent ten minutes scrubbing my footprint from the vanity before flushing the toilet to maintain my cover story. I (regretfully) lowered the toilet seat, effectively tampering with the evidence I'd been so happy to spot.

I washed and dried my hands and yanked the door open (with considerable effort and one foot on the wall for leverage.) I hovered on the landing, looking left and right. Peggy appeared at the bottom of the stairs with an empty case of Chardonnay. "I was starting to worry about you," she said.

I descended the stairs and followed her into the study. "We're just about done," Nick said.

"Thank you, Peggy. I'm sure your husband will be pleased when he finds out you cooperated with us. This party is going to be very special to him." I set a football trophy in the bottom of the box and added a deceptively heavy pile of folded garments.

Peggy's expression changed, but it wasn't anger or disgust that took over her features. If I had to bet, I'd say she was nervous. Why? If she thought we'd find something, she wouldn't have let us in. What was it? I felt like we were in front of a clue and didn't even know it.

"I just assumed, after what I've read in the papers about Tradava, that the party was off."

"Your husband's retirement is a milestone. I'm sure you'll enjoy having him around the house and out of the dangerous situations that come with being a homicide detective." It was bait, pure and simple. Peggy hadn't said one thing to indicate she and Loncar were getting divorced or that he didn't live here anymore. She'd accepted every single fabrication we'd offered since arriving, including a lie about someone from Tradava having called ahead. Her willingness to play along was suspicious.

Nick put his hand on my arm, and I stopped talking. He knew something. Either that or he had an unexpected desire for a public (ish) display of affection.

"I hate to rush you out, but I do have to attend to the baby," Peggy said.

A male voice called down the stairs. "It's okay, Peg. I finally got her to sleep." Footsteps came closer, and the door to the study opened. Whoever Peggy Loncar was with was about to give himself up.

He entered and seemed surprised to find Nick and me in the room. Recognition hit me as quickly as it dawned on him. I forced a smile, though I was anything but happy.

"Samantha?" the man asked.

"Captain Valderama?"

25

COVER BLOWN

"Samantha?" Peggy repeated. "You introduced yourself as Mrs. Taylor."

Nick stepped closer and put his arm around my shoulders. "She *is* Mrs. Taylor. I'm Nick Taylor, and she's my wife."

Peggy ignored Nick. "What is your name?" she asked me.

It would have been a good time to lie, but Captain Valderama removed the opportunity. "Her name is Samantha Kidd."

Nick had been right. Peggy recognized my name. "Get out," she said. She pointed to the door. I picked up the box. She put her hands on her hips. "Really?" she asked.

"But I thought—"

"You thought wrong. Get out and tell my ex-husband it didn't work."

"Your ex-husband doesn't know we're here," Nick said.

While Peggy turned to glare at Nick, I locked eyes with Captain Valderama. He'd been the one to ask me to plan Loncar's surprise retirement party. He could easily tell Peggy that I was there on his request. And if he wasn't there because of the detective, then why *was* he there? Valderama broke eye contact and looked away. I tried to process what was happening, but there were too many competing questions.

I set the box on the corner of the desk. Nick moved closer to it, and the box tipped. It landed on the green carpet, spilling out trophies and framed certificates.

"There's nothing in there that doesn't rightfully belong to Detective Loncar," I said. "Your desire to hold on to his personal items seems to contradict your need to cut all ties from him. You may want to think about what that says about you and your rush to dissolve your marriage." I walked out of the room.

All I'd wanted was to get in a jab, to make a statement on Loncar's behalf. I didn't know whether he was responsible for his marriage falling apart, but right now, all I saw was a bitter woman who was trying to punish someone she once claimed to love. And if that sort of behavior kept Peggy Loncar from finding true love, then she was going to have to accept a long and lonely life.

Except maybe Peggy wasn't looking for true love.

Maybe true love had found her right here in her ex-husband's house.

Peggy and Captain Valderama?

All the questions that had been floating around my brain fell neatly into custom-shaped holes. Why the captain was enforcing Loncar's mandatory retirement. Why Peggy was pressing for the divorce now. Why she wanted the party canceled, and why she wanted us out of the house.

They both wanted Loncar out of the picture. If Loncar retired, he'd have no reason to keep showing up at the police station. When word leaked about Peggy and Valderama's relationship, it would circle through the contained audience of cops. Loncar would be on the outside. The papers would be signed, and he'd be the bad guy who cheated on his wife. She'd get half of his pension, the house, and whatever else she demanded.

Even if she'd cheated too.

I was so lost in my thoughts that I reached the front door and realized I was alone. No one, not even Nick, had followed me out of the office. I turned away from the front door and spotted the entrance to the kitchen.

Loncar had wanted me to look at a planner on a table in the kitchen.

It was where he said it would be. The planner was open to January. I flipped through the pages until I reached April and scanned the entries. One stood out.

10 a.m. Tradava.

The day of the shooting.

I flipped to the front of the planner and found Peggy Loncar's name neatly written on the front page.

What business did Peggy Loncar have at Tradava the day of the shooting? And who else knew she'd been there?

I picked up the planner to get a better look and heard voices. I opened my navy-blue handbag, dropped the planner inside, and closed the handles. I ran across the living room and had my hand on the doorknob to leave when I heard Nick's voice. "Thank you, Peggy. I'll explain everything to my wife."

He rounded the corner with the chardonnay box. I held the door open for him, and he walked out. "Let's get out of here."

He set the box on the seat between us, and we left with Peggy Loncar and Captain Valderama watching us from inside Loncar's house.

We were three blocks away when Nick spoke. "What did you take?"

"You think I took something? From their house?" I asked with somewhat inauthentic damaged pride. "You think I'm a thief?"

"I think you set that box on the corner of Loncar's desk to buy some time. I think I knocked it over to see if they were more interested in following you or seeing what it was we had taken. I certainly hope if you found something, you took it. Otherwise, I'll have to replace the frame on Loncar's Hall of Fame certificate for nothing."

"Does it have his first name?"

Nick looked away from the road at me and then back at the road. "Yes, it has his first name on it. Did you think his first name was 'Detective'?"

"I don't know." I held up my hands palm-side out. "I don't want to know. Once I start thinking of him with a first name, then I stop thinking of him as Detective Loncar. He's being forced out of the job that defines him, and that's sad. I want to remain in the part of his life where he's Detective Loncar. The part of his life that he chose."

Nick reached across the seat and took my hand. "Have I ever told you I love how you think?"

I told Nick about the planner and pulled it out of my handbag. Anger bubbled up inside me. Anger on behalf of Detective Loncar. How dare Peggy move on to Loncar's boss after Loncar had made a life for her? How dare she?

And even worse was the creeping knowledge that Peggy Loncar and Captain Valderama were more connected to the shooting than I'd wanted to think. The captain had been the one to send Loncar to Tradava that morning. He'd been the one to arrange for the surprise party. He'd pulled strings to get us all at the same place, and an innocent person who'd been at the wrong place at the wrong time had died.

And if I was right and Captain Valderama and Peggy Loncar had something to do with the shooting, then there was another casualty: my alter ego, Mrs. Taylor. Because my actions in Loncar's house had officially broken her unblemished record of steering clear of criminal investigations.

26

MANIFESTING REINFORCEMENTS

WE ARRIVED BACK at my house. I immediately manifested reinforcements (Eddie and food). (Manifesting is easy when you have a cell phone.) Nick set the table while I updated the whiteboards with what we'd learned.

Eddie showed up with two pizzas. "You're not still eating fish and chips, are you? I've hit my limit on fried cod."

"You and me both."

I took the boxes and opened the top one. I inhaled the scent of cheese and tomato for a count of four, held my breath and exhaled in a whoosh. The breathing technique was more satisfying with the scent of pizza under my nose. I repeated two times.

My world was righting itself.

Except I was no closer to understanding what had happened at Tradava two days ago.

We went into the kitchen, and I grabbed the oregano and the crushed red pepper from the cabinet and set them on the table. "Two pizzas? I only manifested one."

"Dude," Eddie said. He flipped the top box open. "I asked Xavier to join us."

Nick looked up. "Who's Xavier?"

"One of my freelancers," Eddie said. He turned to me. "His brother owns a landscaping business. The two of them have mad skills, and they're going to build the miniature English topiary maze Moneypenny wanted us to build in the parking lot. We can repurpose it for Loncar's thing."

Nick looked from Eddie to me. "Who's Moneypenny?"

"Victoria," I said. "British sales executive from Piccadilly. I told you about her when we left Peggy's house."

"Who's Peggy?" Eddie asked.

"Detective Loncar's ex-wife," Nick said.

Nick and Eddie looked at me. Each man had half of the story.

"Pizza first. Then we recap."

We claimed one pizza for ourselves and gave the other to Eddie's freelancers. Nick and Eddie got a head start while I doused mine in oregano, but in pizza eating, I'm practically an Olympian, and I caught up quickly.

Between slices, I picked up the red marker and turned to the blank dry erase board. Along the top, I wrote SUSPECTS.

"There was a shooting outside Tradava. Two victims: Harvey Monahan and Detective Loncar. Which means either the shooting was about one or the other."

"You're right back where you started," Eddie said.

"You two were there the morning of the shooting, right?" Nick asked. Eddie and I nodded. "Tell me everybody who you remember."

"Victoria," I said. "She and I were working in the parking lot. She went inside with Harvey to negotiate a deal. The human resources manager told me they never made it to his office. Harvey came back out and was shot. Turns out Harvey has dirt on Victoria and blackmails her to get results on his strikes."

"How do you know that?" Eddie asked.

"She told me." I looked back and forth between their faces. "I'm a natural at female bonding."

"Write her on the board," Eddie said.

I wrote VICTORIA PRATT.

"Next?" Nick asked.

Eddie helped himself to a second piece of pizza. "Taryn Monahan," he said.

"Harvey's sister?" I asked. "Why would she shoot her brother?"

"I'm not concerned with motive right now. I'm giving up suspects."

I wrote TARYN MONAHAN.

"Izzy Smalls was there," I said.

Nick's brow furrowed. "Who's Izzy Smalls?"

"The lead singer of The Ex-Pistols. They were playing at the whiskey bar, remember? I wanted to hire them for Loncar's party."

"Wanted to?"

"Victoria said no."

"Izzy was at Tradava?" Eddie asked. "I never saw her, and she doesn't exactly blend in."

"She told me she was there. She said her ex arranged to meet her to pay back some money he owed her, but it turned out he had no intention of paying her back."

"Either she was lying, or somebody wanted her to be there," Nick said. "Any idea who her ex is?"

"A cop," I said. "His name is Bob Pennino. If we believe her, then she places him at Tradava during the shooting too."

"Do we believe her?" Eddie asked.

"I don't know. She threw a beer on him at Whiskey Mick's right before I talked to her." I leaned back against the wall. Bob Pennino of the porno mustache and the heavy build had been among the more vocally antagonistic in the lobby of the hospital the night I went to visit Loncar.

I wrote IZZY SMALLS and BOB PENNINO.

"Who else was there?"

"John Jones, the human resource manager at Tradava," I said.

Eddie said, "He was inside the store. All members of senior management were. Why did you single him out?"

"Because he said Harvey and Victoria never made it to his office, but he knew they'd reached an agreement on negotiations. How would he know that?"

We tossed theories and suspects around for the better part of an hour. We finished the pizza and put a dent in the blueberry pie. I felt no closer to the truth.

Jet lag was having its way with Nick, and Eddie was distracted by a game of laser tag with Logan, who'd joined us.

I couldn't sit still. "I'm going to Tradava," I said. I took Nick's keys and left.

———

I DROVE to Tradava and parked next to the *Ribbon Eagle/Times* news van. Frank Mazurkiewicz leaned against the front watching a video on his phone. The security team was down to a thin, middle-aged man with two days' beard growth and a black man with chrome-rimmed glasses. Five members of the union strike/candlelight vigil stood by the front doors.

Taryn Monahan had her back to me. She wore a dusty-rose quilted bomber jacket with a short black skater skirt peeking out below, black tights, and pink-and-black argyle over-the-knee socks with Pink UGG boots. She shot me a dirty look over her shoulder and turned back to her group. Without thinking, I held my hands up in a "what did I do?"

gesture, which was lost on her since she wasn't looking.

"Hey, Samantha," Frank said. "Just can't stay away, can you?"

"I'm not here for Tradava. I'm here for you."

"Me?"

"Yes. You've been here every day since the shooting, right?"

"Right."

"And you've been writing stories about it for the paper, right?"

"Right."

"And has anybody from Tradava come out to make a statement? Or offer condolences? Or, well, anything?"

"Nope."

"Nope. That's what I thought." I stared at the façade of the building. The large, concrete structure had remained relatively unchanged since it had been built in the forties: a broad building with a flat roof and a bottle-green "T" mounted on the left side next to the Tradava logo. Massive green-tinted windows and glass panels framed the entrance. I still remembered how it had felt to walk through those doors when I was a little girl, to enter, and look up at the ceiling with the hanging brass sculptures that decorated the atrium before passing through the second set of customer doors.

Harvey had expected the strike to last a week at most. And because of the shooting, the store was going to close.

The news about Piccadilly pulling their funding should have shut them down, but they were still there.

We were a week past the targeted strike resolution. That meant a full week's worth of payroll that had been quietly accumulating on the balance sheets. Payroll that Tradava had diverted into a slush fund that John Jones could pay at his discretion . . . if only there were a job for these people to do.

"Is your cameraman here?" I asked Frank.

"No, he got called to cover a water main break in Antietam," he said. "If anything happens, I'm supposed to film what I can with my phone."

"That'll have to do. Let's go."

Frank followed me into the store and didn't ask questions. I accepted his silence as a vote of confidence in my actions and said as much while we were riding the Up escalator. "Carl would have demanded to know what I had in mind before following me. I appreciate your faith in my actions."

Frank shrugged. "It's less faith than boredom."

You work with what you get.

We reached the fifth floor. Before I opened the door, I turned to Frank. "Turn on your video camera and record this. Make sure the bald guy knows you're recording him, and whatever happens, don't let him take your phone away."

"It's personal property. I don't work for Tradava. If he took my phone, that would be stealing."

"Good. Yes. That is the right way to think. Now the last time I talked to John, he was friendly, but to be honest, I'm not sure how this is going to go. Are you ready?"

"You're in charge."

I entered Human Resources with Frank on my heels. "Hello?" I called out. Two doors were open, but no people were present. "John? Are you here?"

John Jones came out of his office. "Samantha. And . . . do I know you?"

"John, this is a representative of the media. He's recording this for a story about Tradava. I have a few questions, and I suggest you think carefully about your answers."

"You got a job at the newspaper?"

"No," I said. "This is a public interest story." Frank aimed his phone at me. I jerked my head twice toward John, and after I felt satisfied the camera was filming the correct subject, continued. "Earlier this week, members of Tradava's newly formed union went on strike. They expected that strike to last three days. It's been over a week now, and thanks to the shooting and the act of God clause, Tradava is going out of business. That money, that payroll is going to get whooshed away with the rest of the assets around here, but it's not an asset. It belongs to the employees."

"The employees were on strike. Technically they didn't do their jobs, so they haven't earned their pay."

"Is that the position you want to take?" I asked.

John sighed. "What is it you want, Samantha? It's five minutes to six, and these days I see no reason to work a minute longer than I need to." He held his hands out palm side up and bent his fingers toward him. "Give me your bottom line."

I hadn't expected John to roll over quite this easily, and for a moment I was thrown off by his agreeability. Frank pointed his phone at me. "What is your bottom line, Samantha?" he said, presumably to liven up the video.

I turned back to John. "You told me Tradava left you a slush fund for payroll to cover the gap before Piccadilly took over the payroll. Something about money set aside that was protected from debt collectors. Find a way to access that payroll and divert it into an account that I can access."

"You're blackmailing me?"

"It's not blackmail when it's the right thing. Did you ever stop to consider how much this store owes people? Or were you planning on keeping that money for yourself?"

A chair shifted from inside John's office. We weren't alone. And then Peggy Loncar appeared in the doorway. "Give her the money, John," she said. "Samantha already knows I was here the morning of the shooting. She thinks I'm a suspect in my husband's shooting. She'll expose our secrets while searching for the truth."

27

NOT PROUD

THINGS HAD TAKEN a turn for the weird. I looked at her, and at John, and back at her. Something that John had told me the last time I was here niggled at me. He'd told me his connection to Loncar. Neighbors. Friends. Him not wanting to be the cause of more friction between Loncar and his wife.

More friction.

"Of course. You two know each other," I said slowly. "If you crashed on Loncar's sofa, then you two—" I moved my finger back and forth between them, "aren't strangers."

"I'm not proud of what I did, and I'd hoped it would never come out. We both did."

"That's why you stayed over that night," I said to John. "You were separated, but Peggy wasn't. You and Peggy—"

I turned to her. "You cheated on Detective Loncar with his friend?"

"He knew," she said. "He knew I wasn't happy, and he knew I turned to John. When he went out in search of John that night, it wasn't to make sure John made it home safely. He wanted to confront him. I tried to stop my husband, but he was too angry."

My brain fast-tracked the distance between the points of fact. John left and tripped the silent alarm at Loncar's house. Loncar went after John to put a stop to the affair. Vandals choosing that night to break into John's house. Loncar's cop instincts took over, and he pushed everything out of his head except for getting John's ex-wife out of the house. He saved her life, and because of the unbelievable emotional drain of the night, everybody moved on as if resolution had been met.

I kept my attention on Peggy. "Have you told anybody about this?"

"It was years ago. I've tried to forget it. It wasn't until I learned that Tradava was to be the site of my ex-husband's retirement party that I came here to stop your plans. None of us need a reminder of what could have been." She wrung her hands. "My ex-husband has made a lot of enemies in his time on the police force. It's a dangerous job. I told him he had to choose between me and the job, and he chose the job."

"You kicked him out," I said.

"I gave him time to think."

"He wanted to reconcile."

"Samantha, his choice of the job over his marriage wasn't just about him. It was about me too. Why do you think Captain Valderama was at my house earlier today?"

I had a definite theory about that, but now didn't seem the time to mention it. I tried not to react one way or the other, but I could not be held responsible for the judgmental aspects of my body language.

"I got tired of being shunned when I go to the grocery store. I got tired of attending events without my plus one. I raised our daughter while my husband worked eighty-hour weeks. I didn't choose that life. He did."

"You had to know when you married him what your life was going to be like," I said.

"That wasn't the life we agreed on. He went through the academy and moved up from uniform to homicide. The plan was for him to take a desk job. But his priorities changed. We both deserve to be happy, but that doesn't mean I want anything less for him."

"Then why did you send your divorce papers to him at the precinct? Why do something so passive aggressive?"

"I did nothing of the sort," she said, clearly offended at the insinuation. "We had coffee at the Wyomissing Diner. He met his granddaughter for the first time. We shared a slice of pecan pie. It was all very civilized."

"But the rumors I heard said you humiliated him. You

wanted to make a point about his affair with the dispatch officer."

The color drained from Peggy's face. "What affair?"

"Did I say affair? I meant mentorship. There wasn't anything going on between them."

"What is this woman's name?" Peggy asked. Her voice was strained, and when I glanced at her hands, I saw they were balled so tightly the skin over her knuckles had turned white.

I looked at Frank. He had the iPhone aimed at me, and I quickly turned away. This video shakedown had not gone as anticipated. "Does her identity matter? You know your husband."

"Ex-husband."

I ignored her correction. "You know him. Just look at what you told me tonight. He knew about you and John, and he didn't let it destroy your marriage. I don't know when that happened, but you two stayed together, so he must have forgiven you."

"My husband shut down," she said quietly. "He threw himself into his job. It was like I no longer existed." She shifted her attention from me to John, and as she continued talking, I felt like an eavesdropper on a heart-wrenching conversation that should have been private. "I thought—for a very long time, I thought the threat to your wife that night made you rethink everything. I thought you chose her over me. I was ready to leave my marriage like we discussed, and then you just cut ties."

I turned to John. "That's why you never met with Victoria and Harvey for negotiations. You were already in a meeting with Peggy."

"If they were here, I didn't see them." He turned to Peggy. "That night changed everything. What could have happened, it haunts me. That's why I stopped calling. Every time I thought about you, about us, I thought about how many people could have been hurt by our actions."

"But they weren't," she said. "All these years, we turned away from something that could have been great because of something that never took place."

"Just because no one was physically hurt doesn't mean there wouldn't have been pain."

While the four of us stood there, a knock sounded on the glass door to Human Resources. I turned and saw two security guards in uniform. Bob Pennino pulled the door open and poked his head inside. "Mr. Jones, we're here for the six o'clock shift. You want us out front or out back?"

John left the three of us and walked to the door. The office was small, and I could still hear them even though they'd put distance between us. "Did anybody show up tonight?" John asked.

The portly cop-turned-security officer scratched his mustache. "Not yet. Do you want me to stick around? Captain Valderama offered me a pickup shift downtown."

"No, that's not necessary." John and Bob shook hands.

"Protecting lives is more important than protecting a store full of merchandise."

"Got it." Bob adjusted the brim of his hat. He looked over his shoulder, first at me and then at Frank, who appeared to be playing a virtual football game on his phone. Bob leaned in close to John and said something I couldn't hear. John turned his head slightly to the side as if checking to see if I was watching him. I quickly picked up a snow globe with a miniature Tradava from the corner of John's desk and shook it. Glittery snow fell around the miniature department store. I'd watched customers stare at these like they were the most fascinating things they'd ever seen. (The effect wasn't half bad, I must admit.)

While John and Bob finished, I let my mind wander to John's relationship with Peggy. If John Jones had stayed at Loncar's house, the two thugs who broke in would have found his wife, and who knows what they would have done. Peggy Loncar was talking about a love affair that never got started, and John was talking about the human condition.

John was right. There was too much baggage attached to something that hadn't yet begun. It would never have worked.

Peggy went back into his office. A moment later, John followed. I heard a tissue being pulled out of a box, and very faint sounds of crying. Everything about this party for Loncar had turned sour.

Who was I kidding? I planned the entire party based on a Spice Girls ticket stub I found in the bottom of a box of his personal items. I'd picked my theme based on convenience. Unless I gave him a time machine and a sex change, Loncar wouldn't appreciate a Spice Girls-themed party. I'd taken the easy way out because it was easy, and it had brought me nothing but trouble.

I'd discovered more about Loncar's life than I ever thought I wanted to know. He'd experienced loss and pain and a broken heart. And through all of that, he'd found a way to do his job. Even when people like me complicated things.

I turned to Frank. "You can turn off the phone now," I said.

"Already did." He closed the football app and looked up. "You did good," he said.

"It doesn't feel that way. I came here to get answers from John, but he answered questions I wasn't even asking."

"After all that, you still have questions?"

"Two people were shot outside Tradava. I don't know which one was the target and which was the accidental victim. I'm spinning in circles, and nothing's coming together."

"Maybe that's not your job."

"What do you mean?"

"You're confused because you were there when it happened, right?"

"Right."

"And you've got a whole lot of suspects who seem unrelated, right?"

"Right."

"But they were all here too. Maybe that's important. Find a way to get them all together and see what happens."

"How am I supposed to do that?"

"For starters, you can throw that party for Loncar."

"There's no budget, no location, and no guest list. He doesn't even want the party I was planning."

"It's not too late to change your plans. Throw the party you think the detective wants and invite the public."

"What are you suggesting? That I throw a rave in the parking lot?" At Frank's raised eyebrows, I added, "not that I think Loncar wants a rave."

"People love a feel-good story," Frank said. "Sometimes they're moved to do things they might not otherwise do."

Frank wasn't just making small talk. The hopelessness I felt about the party, the out-of-work employees, Loncar's unwanted mandatory retirement, and the lack of support from Tradava faded. A flicker of possibility lit within me. "What do you have in mind?"

"Policeman shot on the site of a long-loved, now dying, formerly owned family retailer affects a community. All you need is the right story and the right media outlet to make people feel what you feel."

"But people don't like cops. When I moved here, *I* didn't like cops."

"But you like Loncar."

"Because I found out he's not just a cop."

Which was precisely the point Frank was trying to get me to see.

John cleared his throat behind me. "The parking lot is available," he said. "I could reallocate the slush fund and approve billable hours from our existing staff," he said. "If we're going out, we might as well go out with a bang."

28

INTERRUPTING MY MOJO

I SENT Frank on his way to get started on the article, and I doubled back to the candy department and checked for the cases of Jacob's Twiglets. Six of them were in a pile behind the counter with a sign that said, "Waiting on Return Authorization."

I tore off the sign and ejected a long strip of register tape and wrote, "Do not return to vendor. Mark out of stock and deliver to advertising office for Loncar Retirement Party." I wandered around the store and left similar notes on the Hello London! handbags, the Keep Calm sweaters, and a box of red-and-blue plaid umbrellas. It was like a scavenger hunt throughout the dark store, identifying any merchandise that could be used in a makeshift American in London pop-up shop. I was beyond caring about the authenticity of the event. Victoria could take her snooty tea and bugger off.

By the time I left the store, the parking lot was vacant. Six metal poles and the massive Union Jack were the only indications that something was to take place in the parking lot. There was no sign of the vigil for Harvey or security for the building. It was ironic that as Tradava slowly died their inevitable death, the one person who seemed to care was me.

I got into Nick's truck and drove home.

Since the shooting, I focused on the tragedy. But before the tragedy, there'd been a party for a man. And if I'd learned anything by now, it was that life was short and the unexpected happened. Detective Loncar wasn't a perfect man, but he'd spent his life trying to protect others. He deserved the celebration, and I was going to give it to him.

When I got home, I was brimming with enthusiasm and ideas. I burst through the door and found Eddie stretched out on the sofa watching *Spice World* and Nick at the dining room table with a sketch pad and swatches of leather. Xavier and a man I didn't recognize were repotting a plant in the middle of my kitchen. I admit, his presence interrupted my mojo.

"Dude," Eddie said. "That's Xavier's brother Juan."

"Hi, Juan," I said.

"Hey. You shouldn't let the roots get so crowded in the pot."

I gave Eddie a confused look. He shrugged. "Listen to the man. He knows plants."

"Good. Because I'm going to need that English topiary maze." I paused and looked at all three of them. "And a miniature Stonehenge. And a tea service and biscuits and models in Geri dresses and goodie bags filled with Twiglets."

"Twiglets?" Eddie asked.

"England's answer to pretzels. And we'll move all the TVs from the electronics department outside and stream Bond movies. And Hugh Grant! What was I thinking? We can't have a party without him. There's got to be someone who can figure that out, right?" I unwound my red scarf from my neck and tossed it on the arm of the sofa. "We need goodie bags. We can fill them on site."

"Who's we?" Eddie asked.

"Anybody who works for Tradava until they officially close their doors."

"Does she always talk this fast?" Xavier asked.

Eddie waved his hand to shush Xavier, and Nick smiled. "She's just getting warmed up," he said.

"We need the maze and chairs and a stage. And models. Can we get employees to model?" I didn't wait for an answer. "And food. Maybe we can get a sponsor? I'll call The Ex-Pistols—"

"Dude, you're scary right now," Eddie said. He turned to Nick. "She wasn't like this before you married her."

Nick held up his hands. "Don't put this on me."

XAVIER INVOKED the union worker's phone tree and spread the word to the other out-of-work employees. I left Eddie wrestling some chicken wire into Stonehenge and Nick in charge of procuring the Geri dresses (which frankly I didn't hold out much confidence in getting, but go big or go home, right?). We were charging full steam ahead. There was just one person who needed to know what I was up to, and that conversation was better in person.

I drove to the hospital and breezed through the visitor sign-in station. Tonight, the lobby was empty. Whether it was because Loncar was out of the woods or because crime stops for nobody, I didn't know. I was just happy not to be harassed.

I reached Loncar's room and tapped on the door-frame. "Hi," I said.

Loncar glared at me. From that single expression, annoyance with a side of vinegar, I knew he somehow learned that the party was on.

"Hear me out," I said. I grabbed the closest chair and sat facing him. "A lot of people are out of work thanks to that shooting. The shooting led to Piccadilly Group pulling out of their deal to buy Tradava, and now Tradava is filing for bankruptcy. The money was there for payroll, but because of the strike, nobody was showing up for work. This party will get those people paid, and it'll show Piccadilly what they should have seen all along—that Tradava is a good bet."

"You're using me."

"Sort of. Yes." I paused a moment. "Is that a problem?"

"I didn't expect you to own up to it so quickly."

"I'm on an adrenaline high."

Loncar crossed his arms over his hospital gown. (They really should make those things out of more sturdy fabric.) I leaned back in my chair and stared off at the window. I could sit here and let him be Cranky Loncar to my I-can-do-this! Samantha, but it felt wrong not to acknowledge everything I'd learned about him.

"I have to ask you something personal," I said. "You don't have to answer me, but it would help my investig—" Loncar shot me a warning look—"it would help me figure something out."

"What?"

"How did your wife deliver your divorce papers?" I held my breath and waited for an answer (or a phone call to the front desk to revoke my visitor privileges).

Loncar stared at me. He didn't throw me out, but his silence may have been a preemptive verbal strike against further personal questions.

"We went to lunch at the Wyomissing Diner," he finally said. "She brought my granddaughter." He shrugged, looked at his hands, and then at me. "Maybe it was to soften the blow. I don't know. I don't know why she did it that way. But the writing was on the wall. No point trying to force my company on somebody who didn't want me around."

His version varied from his wife's in anecdotal style, but the facts remained the same. The rumors Detective Madden had relayed at Whiskey Mick's were just that—rumors. It made me wonder what else I'd heard that had been fabricated for my benefit. Or for someone else's.

It also made me realize how well I'd gotten to know Detective Loncar while he lay in this bed. Going through his office, talking to his friends, rifling through the box Geri had given me for inspiration. He was like a final exam, and I'd studied like a senior with one grade between me and graduation.

I would never again be able to circumvent the system while trying to figure out a crime myself. Loncar getting shot had done the unthinkable. It had made me understand why we left the criminal investigations to the police.

"I know about Peggy and John," I said quietly. "I know about the break-in and affair and the reason you went out after John when he left in the middle of the night."

"How?"

He wasn't asking who told me or where I'd come across the information. He wanted to know what breadcrumbs I'd followed to obtain that knowledge.

"Short version or long version?"

"Long."

"I went to your house. I told your wife I was there to pick up some of your personal belongings to use in a display at the party. She let me into your study—"

"Peggy knows who you are. She wouldn't have let you into the house."

"I may have used a fake name. A real fake name. I mean a fake real name. I mean—"

"Who?"

"Mrs. Taylor," I said. Loncar raised his eyebrows, and the tiniest smile crept onto his face. "Nick was with me. He packed a box of stuff while I tried to see what I could, um, ascertain from her current living quarters."

"You were snooping."

"You could say that."

"And you found something."

"Someone flushed the toilet when we got there, and when I used the same bathroom, the seat was up," I said. "I knew a man was there. Well, I guess I didn't know that for sure, but between Peggy and the baby, I doubt there was a need to lift the toilet seat."

"Valderama," he said.

"You knew?"

"I asked Madden to have someone on the force keep an eye on her. In case this was about me. He told me Valderama made the visits himself. Is that it?"

"I climbed onto the sink to listen at the vent but the heater went on, and my ear got hot." He glared at me. "Oh, you mean did I find out anything else?" He nodded. "There was a notation on the calendar in the kitchen. An appointment at Tradava. Monday at 10. That's when the shooting took place. I never saw her, and I couldn't figure out why she'd be there, but then I remembered the story John told me. If John crashed on your sofa, then he crashed on Peggy's sofa."

"Tell me what made you put it together."

I dropped my eyes to my hands in my lap. "John said he left that night because he didn't want to put more pressure on your marriage. He used the word 'more.' And the way he said it, I knew. John was the source of the strain. You knew he had an affair with Peggy, and you still let him crash on your sofa."

Loncar looked away from me and stared out the window. He didn't say I was wrong.

"I went to Tradava tonight to convince John to use the payroll slush fund to pay people to work on your party. Peggy was in his office. She knew I took the planner from her house, and she wanted to warn him that I thought she was a suspect. She knew I'd find out the truth."

Loncar's head whipped back toward me. "You stole the planner from my house?"

"I was startled and I dropped it."

"Where?"

"Into my handbag."

"Ms. Kidd."

"Detective Loncar," I said before he could launch into a lecture. "This isn't about me trying to ID the shooter. It's about me planning a retirement party, which you told me to keep planning so I could get into your house. You wanted me to find out where your wife was the morning of the shooting, and to find that out, I had to look at her planner."

"There is a difference between looking and taking."

"Tomato, tomahto."

"We may have reached a point where you need to learn the rules of investigative work."

"Are they actual rules? I figured they were more like guidelines."

Loncar rubbed his face. "If you quote *Pirates of the Caribbean* again, I'm going to arrest you."

"And then you'll lose your connection to the case. I got the intel you needed."

"Ms. Kidd, you are a private citizen planning a party. You are not a spy."

People seemed to get hung up on that.

"You're right," I said. "I'm planning a party. Everybody knows that. And that party has opened doors. And you can't tell me to stop anymore because we're past that. It may seem like the party is for you, but it's also for the community. It's for the people who stood vigil outside Tradava after the shooting. It's for Frank Mazurkiewicz, the sports reporter for the *Ribbon Eagle/Times* who has been covering this investigation while Carl Collins is on vacation. It's for Harvey and Taryn Monahan, who unionized the support staff at the store because they believed those workers deserved something better. It's for Detective Madden, who needs to make some friends if he's going to stay in Ribbon. And it's for your daughter Geri, who told me who she was named after."

Loncar blushed. "She didn't."

"She did. And the idea that your daughter is named after a Spice Girl says more about you than I've learned since I moved back to Ribbon."

I stood up and buttoned my jacket. There was one more thing I needed to find out, and it would save me a lot of time if I could ask. But it involved Loncar's affair with Bridget MacDugal, and that was dangerously close to asking him about his sex life. I tried to act nonchalant while I worked up my nerve. There was no easy way to ask so I finally just blurted it out.

"What made you think it was a good idea to cheat on your wife with someone from the force?"

29

I COULD DO THIS ALL DAY

WHATEVER LONCAR HAD EXPECTED me to ask, that wasn't it. His eyes flashed dark and angry, and the machine behind his bed beeped in double time.

"Who told you that?" he asked.

"Is it true?"

"Who told you that?"

"Is it true?" (I could do this all day.)

"Who told you that?" (Apparently he could too.)

"Detective Madden told me. He said your wife had your divorce papers sent to the precinct. I assumed it was because she found out about your affair with Bridget and wanted to make a point, but then I found out the rumors were just that. Rumors. Peggy wanted out, and your divorce was civilized. Why do the cops all believe something else?"

"This is about Bridget?" he asked. Something passed

over his expression. It was a flash that shifted his features from annoyance to surprise. He narrowed his eyes and stared at the foot of his bed, and then his expression morphed into understanding. He grabbed the bars on the side of the bed and tapped his open left hand against the plastic, making a *tap tap tap* sound with his wedding ring.

Loncar did this. He spun his ring or tapped his desk or clicked the ends of pens or bounced his thumb against his space bar. It meant he was thinking. It was one of his more annoying habits, but while he'd been lying in this hospital bed, I'd wondered if he was ever going to start doing it again.

I stared at his hand while it made the *tap tap tap* sound, and a surge of emotions rose within me. Detective Loncar—the detective Loncar I knew—was back. All he needed was his old, poorly fitting wardrobe and his orthopedic shoes. I never thought I'd miss his orthopedic shoes.

The detective's eyes opened wide, and he sat up. His hand went still on the metal bar next to the bed. The machine behind his bed let out a piercing alarm, and he clutched his chest. He collapsed against the pillows. Four doctors came into the room and pushed me out of the way. I stood back while they lowered his bed and pushed buttons on the machine and checked the medication flowing into the stent in his arm. I stepped backward once, then twice, then turned and left. Whatever I'd said to trigger that response was the key to everything. It was the reason there'd been a shooting at Tradava, and Detective Loncar knew it. He'd solved the case.

And if he slipped back into his coma, he'd be the only one to know the truth.

I called Nick from the car. "I just left the hospital," I said. "Everything Peggy Loncar told us was true. Somebody wants Loncar's colleagues to think he was sleeping with Bridget, the dispatch officer, but he wasn't. And when I asked Loncar about it, he had a relapse."

I could hear noise in the background, the result of having a house filled with out-of-work employees who'd been given a chance to make the monthly mortgage payment before the reality of unemployment settled in. "Hold on, Kidd," Nick said. The noise faded from the background. "Where are you?"

"I'm driving home. I should be there in fifteen minutes."

"We'll be here. You should see how engaged people are. You're a hero, Kidd."

That was part of the problem. Everybody acted like I'd done some big thing by getting Tradava to pay them, but what if we were all wrong? What if I was sending a group of innocent people back to a crime scene where a shooter had unfinished business? What if this *wasn't* about Loncar? What if Loncar wasn't the intended target and somebody else was still being stalked?

What if what if what if?

I slowed for a yellow light at the end of my street and

waited impatiently at the intersection. All these efforts for the party were either bringing a community together or tearing it apart. I accidentally missed my exit while trying to come to terms with the idea that it was fifty-fifty on which way it would go.

I looped around at the end of the block and drove back to the light and turned left. I couldn't risk making this big of a mistake with potentially fatal consequences. I had to talk to someone, and I knew exactly who to call.

I pulled into the empty Tradava lot and parked in a space in the middle, cut the engine, and turned off my lights. I picked my phone up from the floorboards where it had fallen when I turned around and called *Get PoPT!*

"The power of positive thinking is within your reach. Get popped," answered a bored voice.

"Hi. Long-time listener, first-time caller. I was hoping for some on-air coaching?"

"Name?"

"Samantha. Samantha Kidd."

"Samantha! It's Riley. How are you?"

"Riley?" It took a moment to place the name of the receptionist who had just bought her first pair of Nick's shoes on eBay. "Why are you answering the *Get PoPT!* hotline?"

"Dr. Emma is tonight's expert."

That's why Dr. Emma's voice sounded familiar. I knew her from the podcast!

"Is she broadcasting from the hospital?"

"Yes. Her producer is stuck in traffic. I'm trying to help. What's wrong? Did you—are you—does this have to do with you and Nick?" Riley paused.

"I'm not," I said. "I should say, I wasn't. When I saw you. You were right. But I might be now because Nick and I—never mind."

Riley giggled. "Samantha, if I were married to Nick Taylor, every day would be a 'might be preggers' situation. But that's not why you called. You want to go on the air? Are you sure? This show goes out live to two million listeners and lives on the podcast indefinitely."

Did I want millions of people to know I couldn't make a decision?

Did I honestly believe Dr. Emma, who'd been flummoxed by the choice between mauve, dusty rose, and puce was the person to help me navigate my indecision?

We could go two ways from here: I could cancel the party in fear of a repeat act of violence or I could go forward, reclaim the store and our agenda. Too many good things were on the side of going ahead with the party. Loncar deserved this celebration, and the employees of Tradava deserved this last job.

It was the right thing.

Before I could tell Riley what I'd figured out on my own, my phone buzzed with a text. "Hold on," I said. I looked at the screen and saw a message from Frank Mazurkiewicz. *Need help transcribing audio. Sent file via Dropbox. Deadline 1 hour.*

I deleted the text and returned to the phone call. "You're right," I said to Riley. "I'm going to trust my gut feeling. Would you do me a favor?" I added. "Can you call Nick and tell him I'm on my way home? I'll give you his number."

"Sure!" she said, this time with much more enthusiasm.

I could have made the phone call myself, but the girl deserved something for helping me navigate my crisis.

I hung up and found two files from Frank in my Dropbox. The attached email explained. *Video and audio from today. Can't understand end of conversation. Need quote.*

I remembered him aiming the camera at me, and since I suspected the sight of me on video would distract me from what it was he wanted to know, I opened the audio file instead.

Frank sent a few questions, and I shot back my responses while the audio played. The conversation was interrupted by a knock and then John talking to the security guard about outside security on Tradava. Their voices got low, and I remembered glancing at Frank to see if he was still recording. He'd been playing a video game.

It seemed the VoiceMemo app had been recording in the background.

I fished a pair of earbuds out from the bottom of my handbag and cranked the volume up as high as it would go. I pressed the earbuds deep into my ear canals and closed my eyes and listened. What had Bob asked John after he noticed me?

It was a series of mumbled words. I jumped back fifteen seconds and listened again. And again. And again. I was one hundred percent focused—like Gene Hackman in *The Conversation*—so when someone pounded on my window, I jumped.

Taryn Monahan glared at me.

Tonight, she wore a black parka, black leggings, and black UGG boots. Her hat and mittens were pale pink knit. I rolled down the window far enough to hear her but not enough for her to reach in and possibly strangle me. (I figured I could take her if she tried, but those high kicks I'd seen the first day of the strike suggested she was in better shape than I was.)

"Taryn. Hi. I didn't expect to see you here tonight."

"Nobody else cares anymore. We were doing a good thing, and then you came along and messed everything up."

"But I talked to John. He agreed to pay the support staff to work on the retirement party for Loncar. Didn't Xavier tell you when he called?"

"He said he needed help with a private event and asked me for the phone tree. Is he working for you? For Tradava? They're all working for the store?" Her face turned beet red, and her nose started to run.

Taryn Monahan was not supposed to cry. She was

supposed to become a mean girl, make a snarky comment about me, turn on her heel, and leave. Or possibly try to strangle me through the narrow opening in the window. "Why don't they like me?" she asked. "I've been here every single day and for what? I don't even work for Tradava. My brother said they needed more people, so I showed up to help. I even brought cupcakes with little British flags!" She buried her face in her hands and cried.

I couldn't just let her stand there.

I got out of the truck and put my arms around her. "People like you," I said. "This has been a stressful situation, and it's taken a toll on everybody. Why don't you follow me back to my house and join the team? We could use another set of hands, and I bet you'd be surprised how welcome you'd be."

"I can't," she sobbed. "My son gave me a ride, and I need to be here when he shows up."

"Can't you call him?"

"I dropped my phone in his car!" she wailed. "I'm such a mess! I can't get my life together. What am I going to doooooo?"

Taryn didn't need friends—she needed an appointment with Dr. Emma. "Get in the truck, Taryn. I'll take you to my house and bring you back when your son is scheduled to pick you up."

"For real?" she asked.

"Yes." I unlocked the passenger-side door. "Get in."

She held up her index finger. "Give me a minute. I left my backpack by the front doors."

She jogged away. In the dark, I kept track of her pink knit hat. The hat disappeared behind the bushes to the left of the front doors and then reappeared as she stood back up. She pulled the backpack on one shoulder sling at a time and then held up her hand and waved at me.

And a second figure stepped out from behind the plants. It was a man in dark clothes with a rotund build and a porno mustache. Bob, the security officer. He said something to Taryn, and she pointed to me. He switched on a flashlight and aimed it at me. I sunk into the seat.

But just before my eyes dropped below the dashboard, I saw Taryn raise something into the air and bring it down on Bob's head. It was dark, and my vision was restricted, but I'd swear it was a gun.

30

SITTING DUCK

BOB CRUMPLED TO THE GROUND. Taryn dropped her hand to her side, but I could tell she was still holding the gun. I was a sitting duck in the parking lot, and I'd already lost the element of surprise.

I grabbed my phone and called 911. "This is Samantha Kidd. I'm in the parking lot outside of Tradava. A woman just assaulted a security guard. He needs help, but if I get out of the truck, she might shoot."

"Stay in your car. I'll send help." She hung up.

I felt more helpless than I'd felt in my life. Any action on my part could result in the death of an innocent person. But inaction on my part could result in the death of an innocent person. Talk about indecision. Should I stay or should I go? I was more conflicted than The Clash.

I stared in the direction of the store. Bob's body lay on

the macadam by the front of the store. He hadn't moved since Taryn struck him.

I had to do something. Starting the engine would give me away. Not having the safety of the truck would make me vulnerable. If Taryn didn't pose enough of a threat, my indecision might kill me instead.

Starting tomorrow, I was going to work on that.

I quietly opened the door. The interior light went on. It took seconds to claw the plastic cover off and remove the lightbulb. I shoved my phone into my pocket and climbed out of the truck, resting the door against the frame but not slamming it shut.

I reached into the box of Loncar's belongings and pulled out his long-outgrown Kevlar vest. It was an older model, from Loncar's early days on the force, and hadn't benefitted from the technological advances that made vests lighter and less bulky. It was several sizes smaller than Loncar, and at the time I'd discovered it, I thought it would be funny to showcase the man he was when he first joined the police force.

I slipped off my blazer and pulled the vest over my crown sweater. The vest weighed more than I imagined. My whole torso felt weighted down, and I took a few unsteady steps while trying to get a feel for the additional weight. I stumbled into the upright steel poles that marked off the party quarters in the parking lot.

I rested against the pole and gave myself a pep talk. "Come on, Samantha. Get it together. Help is coming."

Except I knew help wasn't coming. Not before Taryn Monahan realized I was no longer in the car. And before I could reason through why she knocked out Bob, why she shot her brother and Detective Loncar, and why she pretended to be so helpless less than half an hour ago, a crack sounded through the parking lot and tore a hole through the Union Jack over my head.

31

RETAILERS ARE GREEDY

A SECOND BULLET struck the pole behind me. I fell to the ground and scraped the knee of my ivory tights. Two more shots were fired, and I scrambled to the far side of the tent. There was nothing to hide behind. Nothing to give me shelter.

I should have stayed in the truck.

I shoved my phone into my boot. I reached the far pole and undid the cord that held the flag into place above me. When the rope was loosened, the wind caught the corner and flapped it up into the sky. A bullet tore through the stripe in the center of the flag, and it snapped and floated above us both.

How many shots had that been?

I leaned against the tent pole and stared at the building. My phone rang, and in my panic to remain silent, I rejected the call. My thumb slipped, and I activated the voice memo from inside Tradava. John Jones's voice came out, instructing Bob to leave after midnight if no one showed up for the vigil.

A bullet whizzed past my head, and I got into motion.

I stood up and put my hands in the air. "I know it's you, Taryn. I saw you knock out Bob."

The gun came into focus first. It was almost impossible to look away, to follow the line of the gun, up the arm, to Taryn's face.

"Stay out of this, Samantha. It doesn't concern you."

"Who does it concern? Your brother? You killed him. The police? You've shot one and assaulted another. You won't get away with this."

"My brother never trusted me. I had a winning strategy. Force a strike, turn over staff, and bring in a team to help move drugs to new customers. It's worked before, and it would have worked again."

Drugs? The task force. Loncar had suspected this scenario. "Stores have security," I said. "They would have seen what you were doing on their cameras."

"Retailers are greedy. They don't care what you sell as long as the numbers go into the cash register. Haven't you noticed how much gets sold and returned from a new store opening? It works like a charm every single time."

I pieced together what she wasn't telling me. "You hid the drugs in the merchandise? And ring the merchandise up like a sale?"

"I told you my plan was smart. You almost caught me

last week when you bought that stupid Keep Calm sweater. I had to tear the stash from the garment."

"That's why my sweater didn't have tags."

"Oh, now you're Agatha Raisin all of a sudden?"

"So, what? You attach drugs to the garment and ring up the garment? The money goes into the register. If it's credit, you can't touch it, and if it's cash, it would get caught at the end of the day when the registers are balanced."

"The customer brings their item back for a return, and we get the cash before we process the refund. We sell the highest priced items we can find to make sure our customers come back."

"That Keep Calm sweater wasn't that expensive."

She shrugged. "Dime bag."

While neither *Bridget Jones's Diary* nor *Spice World* provided the intel to know how much a dime bag cost, I was pretty sure she'd just insulted my taste.

But it didn't matter. Piccadilly Group had wanted to stock the grand reopening with pricey items to force on customers. She'd believed that the people who shopped that night were predisposed to buy high-ticket items based on reports from previous store openings. If she had listened to me and let me plan a party our customers would have wanted, we would have shut down Taryn and Harvey's plan before anybody got shot.

"You shot your brother," I said.

"The police were onto us. Harvey was a liability."

I looked over my shoulder. "What about your son? What'll he say when he comes to pick you up and sees you holding me at gunpoint?"

"Get with the program, Samantha. There is no son. There is no lost phone. But you're a fixer. You want to help people. The only way to get you off my back was to play the victim."

I'd spent months listening to *Get PoPT!* and working on my personality flaws, and the one thing I'd always considered a strength—my desire to help people—was going to get me killed. Taryn was crazy, and aside from a flapping Union Jack and the metal tent poles jutting up from the parking lot, I had no weapons at my disposal.

I crouched behind the farthest tent pole, knowing with full certainty that my position had done nothing to make me less of a target. I pulled my phone out of my boot and texted the first number. *Call me back*, then pushed my phone across the macadam toward where Taryn stood. Seconds later, my phone rang. Taryn whirled around and shot it. The phone jumped from the impact.

"You," I said. "You were Harvey's sister. Family. Doesn't that mean anything to you?"

She smiled. "Family's overrated." The shadows cast from the flapping Union Jack made her face look cold and blue, and then flushed red.

She pointed her gun into the sky and fired several shots at the spotlight at the edge of the parking lot. At least one bullet hit. She turned and fired at the next clos-est. I didn't believe Taryn was so good of a shot that she could take out targets at random, but her confidence in pulling the trigger indicated she had enough bullets that she didn't care if she missed. And as she picked off the lights, the parking lot grew dark. Black. Blacker than black.

None more black.

The line from *This is Spinal Tap* popped into my brain, in the voice of Eddie doing Christopher Guest doing Nigel Tufnel. I thought about the past four days, how much had passed since then. Nick in China. The pregnancy test. Eddie's miniature Stonehenge. Bridget flinging water on me at Whiskey Mick's. Detective Madden wanting to ask my friend out on a date. Piccadilly pulling their funding and Tradava filing bankruptcy.

I thought of the mundanity of some days and the outrageousness of others. I thought about Detective Loncar at the middle of it all. A man who I'd once avoided the way I avoided horror movies, who had turned out to be as benign as Jack Lemmon. If I were going to die defending someone, he was a worthy choice.

Except—what was I thinking? I didn't want to die!

A short figure separated from the shadows and crept up behind Taryn. My throat went dry, making it difficult to swallow. Taryn closed one eye and sighted me with her pistol. And an arm in a black fringed leather jacket brought a heavy object down on her head.

Taryn dropped to the macadam.

Loncar's football trophy fell to the ground next to him.

And Bridget MacDugal pulled me up from where I leaned against the tent pole and pulled me into a hug.

———

BOB PENNINO REGAINED CONSCIOUSNESS. He secured Taryn Monahan while I waited for the ambulances to arrive. Bridget took off her fringed leather jacket and draped it over the shoulders of my ivory sweater. The three of us waited for the police together. There were no words that could have created more of a bond than the silence.

More police cars arrived at the parking lot of Tradava than I'd ever seen. It was like a red and blue ant invasion —at least that's the thought that ran through my head after being given a healthy dose of painkillers. I was moved from the ground to a wheelchair and covered in a blanket. Muscles I didn't remember using now ached: my biceps, my triceps, my delts. Had it not been for Nick's commitment to our undercover trip to Loncar's house, the two items that made the difference between life and death would not have been in the parking lot with me.

Oh, and Detective Loncar hadn't slipped back into his

coma. He'd closed his eyes to try to decide if he should confide in me that he was working with two cops—Bridget and Bob—to surveil and expose a drug ring that had planned to use Tradava to move drugs, not department store inventory. That the shooting wasn't about him.

Ironically, in a way, it was.

32

ONE WEEK LATER

THE PARTY for Detective Loncar took place in the parking lot outside of Tradava a week later. Between recovery and last-minute details, I met with Frank from the *Ribbon Eagle/Times* to inform his series about the store, the drug ring, the detective, and the community. I figured he'd be happy to get back to his regular assignment when this was all wrapped up. He'd laughed at that. "Stress-free? This was a walk in the park compared to high school sports."

Frank had included a hotline for people to make pledges to offset the expense of the party, and they did. The outpouring of support exceeded anything Piccadilly had budgeted, or Tradava had left in their slush fund. It was enough to throw the British bash of the century.

John Jones made good on his promise to arrange interviews for the employees of Tradava. New reports in fashion industry journals cited a fresh wave of interest in the retailer, but I tuned them out. Nick was moving on with his footwear collection. Loncar was moving forward with his retirement. For the first time since Eddie had started working at Tradava out of art school, he was moving forward with interviews. It was time for me to move on as well.

But not until the party was over.

The police processed the crime scene and released the parking lot. All along, I'd planned to use the tent for Loncar's party. It was unclear whether I could, until John Jones gave me an envelope that Victoria had asked him to deliver. Inside was a letter, neatly typed on Piccadilly Group letterhead, that indicated Piccadilly's buyout offer of the store was pending an internal review, but that permission to use the parking lot while the company made their final decision was granted to me.

Under the letter, in neat cursive handwriting, was a postscript: *Dear Samantha, I'd be honored to help in any way possible. Sincerely, Victoria Pratt.*

It wasn't her fault the union negotiator had been using his position to staff stores with a team to move drugs into neighborhoods where Piccadilly acquired retail real estate. The poor woman had been gobsmacked by the news.

Yet she attended the party anyway and volunteered to staff the tea station. I admired her commitment.

We moved the party to the evening and rented

heaters that stood around the perimeter. Instead of using the tent as a shopping venue, I'd lobbied senior management to mark items out of stock to use in raffle baskets and party favors. I put together an entirely new wardrobe for Detective Loncar's life in retirement and packed it into a navy-blue steamer trunk with tan leather trim. I added a Union Jack luggage tag and had it delivered to his house. I assumed Peggy would make sure he got it.

Nick and Eddie surprised me with a strapless ball gown made from Union Jack parachutes. It was far classier than the micro-mini Ginger Spice dresses I'd instructed the servers to wear.

At the far end of the tent, Eddie anchored a backdrop for The Ex-Pistols while the women set up their equipment. He wore a short-sleeved T-shirt with a Rolling Stones logo over a long-sleeved white T-shirt, white painter's pants with blue and red paint splatters, and his trademark black-and-white-checkered Vans. The backdrop said, "Keep Calm and Party On, Dudes."

Eddie had outdone himself with the decorations. In addition to the topiary maze and the Stonehenge, he'd crafted red phone booths out of refrigerator boxes that held the goodie bags for attendees to take. If the Visual Director thing at Tradava didn't straighten itself out, he could hang out a shingle for party planning.

I stared into the crowds of people, police in uniform, guests and employees in suits and dresses. The hostility I'd felt in the lobby of the hospital had been replaced with what felt like silent respect. I caught Bridget's eyes and smiled. She smiled back. Bob Pennino approached her and handed her a glass of champagne. They both raised glasses to me and drank.

"What a week," Nick said. "I still don't know how you pulled off a party with everything else going on."

"It was the right thing. I never thought about how much work it would be. I just made it happen."

"The power of positive thinking."

I accepted that Nick knew me pretty well, but I'd kept my podcast dependency on the down low. I turned my head and looked up at him. "Why'd you say that?" I asked.

"That's what you used. You believed this was right, and it was." He tightened his embrace. "I'm proud of you. You found a way to make everybody happy."

I relaxed. "Not quite everybody," I said. "Loncar's still being forced to retire."

"Loncar knew, didn't he?"

"Bridget knew—more like she suspected something. She took her suspicions to Loncar, and they worked out a plan. They needed a third person, someone nobody would suspect was working with them."

"Who?"

"Bob. Bridget's ex-husband," I said. "He was already working part-time security shifts, and nobody would question him being at Tradava."

"But Bridget didn't want Bob to get the wrong idea," Nick said.

"No. Bridget got Loncar to agree to let her spread the rumors about them because it was the one way to maintain Bob's distance."

It was such a silly thing. Bridget needed Bob to believe she and Loncar were involved to keep him on task —a task that would uncover how Harvey Monahan was using turnkey retailers to establish a drug trafficking operation. Bridget's animosity toward me was because I threatened her cover story. Bob's was to protect their sting. And all my digging into Loncar's marriage and Peggy's infidelity had led me on a wild-goose chase.

"Both Harvey and Taryn were involved?"

"Yes," I said. "Taryn hasn't been at Tradava for candlelight vigils. She's been here to cover her tracks."

"A lot changed this week," Nick said. He draped his arms around me from behind, and I leaned against him.

"And one big thing didn't," I said.

We hadn't talked any more about the thought that I'd been pregnant, the proof that I hadn't been, and where we stood on the subject. I was no closer to figuring out how I felt about the idea. I could handle killers, but I still didn't know if I was ready to handle a baby.

Nick relaxed his arms and stepped to my side. "Do you want something to drink?" he asked.

I didn't answer right away. I looked into the crowd and spotted Victoria talking with Detective Loncar by the tea station. He wore a navy-blue suit, white shirt, and black dress shoes. His necktie was red. The entire outfit had been in the steamer trunk I'd had delivered to his house.

Victoria's strawberry-blond hair was loose and flipped up at the ends. She wore a navy-blue sweater dress with a Union Jack knitted into the front with navy-blue tights and knee-high red suede boots. Ginger Spice x Parliament. Her peaches-and-cream complexion glowed, and her manner seemed more relaxed than it had been since I'd met her.

Detective Loncar said something, and Victoria laughed. He smiled, and years of misery fell away from his curmudgeonly aura. He stood a little straighter. My eyes dampened, and I reached out for Nick's arm.

"Kidd," he said. He looked confused by my expression, and then followed my gaze to Loncar and Victoria and nodded knowingly. "Looks like he's enjoying the party after all," he said.

At that moment, the festivities were interrupted by a display of fireworks that colored the night sky. Attendees moved outside the tent to get a better view, but I didn't follow. I was happy right where I was.

Victoria turned and smiled. She raised her champagne flute in my direction, and I smiled back.

"The bar is open. How about some champagne to celebrate?" Nick asked.

"Actually . . ." My voice trailed off. I shifted my focus

from the detective and sales executive to Nick and grinned. "I think I'd rather a spot of tea."

EPILOGUE

WANTED

Office assistant for new private investigation firm.

Owned by retired police detective with 25+ years of
experience.

Experience with technology a plus.

Pay: negotiable. Location: Ribbon, Pennsylvania.

Call 1-800-4LONCAR.

Equal Opportunity Employer.

(Former fashion buyers need not apply)

FROM DIANE:

Spending time in Samantha Kidd's world is always filled with nostalgia, but UNION JACKED was even more so. While writing this book, I moved from California back to Pennsylvania to the very real town that served as the inspiration for Samantha Kidd's town of Ribbon. And while I always knew Samantha's version was closer to my memories than reality, I couldn't ignore how much things had changed since I left in 1998.

It was unavoidable for a sense of change to permeate this story. Samantha will always pursue happiness and personal growth (which, not coincidentally, so will I.). And when the bullet struck Detective Loncar at the end of Chapter Three, we both had a moment when we realized how sad it would be to lose the people we once rallied against.

As far as life coaches go, while I believe there are people who can help us all evolve into better versions of ourselves, that didn't feel like the Samantha Way. She'll keep falling down and getting back up and trying to figure things out on her own.

I hope you enjoy this latest installment in Samantha Kidd's story. She'll be back before you know it!

Sincerely,
　　Diane

P.S. A note about reviews: if you enjoyed this book, please leave a review. Reviews help readers find books and series, and Samantha Kidd would love knowing her antics helped bring joy and happiness to more people's lives. No matter how brief or how long, your review makes a difference.

ACKNOWLEDGMENTS

Every book I write has a unique mix of inspiration that leaves its fingerprint on the final product, and *Union Jacked* is no different. Shoptalk members Amy Ross-Jolly, Patricia Gregory, Nadine Peterse-Vrijhof, Sydney Cavero-Egúsquiza, Sheryl Positano Sens, Pat Dupuy, Kara Vaughan Marks, Judy Johnson, Barbara Harrison, Lilia Tanakeyowma, and Shawna Zimmerman Gregg for contributing names of Fish and Chip eateries. Thank you to my sister and brother-in-law for answering the critical questions for this manuscript, like what is the English equivalent to a pretzel? Jordaina Sydney-Robinson for being my writing friend from across the pond. Frank Mazurkiewicz for articles about my swimming career in the eighties for the Reading Eagle/Times. Cara Alwill Leyba for *Style Your Mind*, the best personal growth podcast for women. Geri Halliwell for making tiny little Union Jack dresses a thing. Christopher Guest and Rob Reiner for *This Is Spinal Tap*. The Polyester Posse, for your support. The D.I.A. (You know who you are.) Readers of the Weekly DiVa, who make up my community! And last but very much not least, my parents, for your support, respect, understanding, and never-ending supply of pretzels. I love you all.

ALSO BY DIANE VALLERE

Killer Fashion Mysteries

Designer Dirty Laundry

Buyer, Beware

The Brim Reaper

Some Like It Haute

Grand Theft Retro

Pearls Gone Wild

Cement Stilettos

Panty Raid

Union Jacked

Slay Ride

Tough Luxe

Fahrenheit 501

Stark Raving Mod

Gilt Trip

Ranch Dressing

Murder Italian Style

Madison Night Mysteries

"Midnight Ice" (prequel novella)

Pillow StalkThat Touch of Ink

With Vics You Get Eggroll

The Decorator Who Knew Too Much

The Pajama Frame

Lover Come Hack

Apprehend Me No Flowers

Teacher's Threat

The Kill of It All

Love Me or Grieve Me

Please Don't Push Up the Daisies

The Glass Bottom Hoax

Sylvia Stryker Outer Space Mysteries

Murder on a Moon Trek

Scandal on a Moon Trek

Hijacked on a Moon Trek

Framed on a Moon Trek

Warped on a Moon Trek

Material Witness Mysteries

Suede to Rest

Crushed Velvet

Silk Stalkings

Tulle Death Do Us Part

Sheer Window

Contesting the Wool

Costume Shop Mystery Series

A Disguise to Die For

Masking for Trouble

Dressed to Confess

Mermaid Mysteries

Dead in the Water

Non-Fiction

Bonbons for your Brain

ABOUT THE AUTHOR

National bestselling author Diane Vallere writes funny character-based mysteries with touches of fashion and history. After two decades working in luxury retailing, she traded fashion accessories for accessories to murder. As past president of the national Sisters in Crime organization, she edited the Agatha-Award-winning essay collection *PROMOPHOBIA: Taking the Mystery out of Promoting Crime Fiction* and has contributed a short story to *MURDER A GO-GO: Crime Fiction Inspired by the Music of the Go-Go's*. Diane started her own detective agency at age ten and has maintained a passion for shoes, clues, and clothes ever since.

Find out more at dianevallere.com.

DIANE VALLERE

where style meets sleuthing

or visit
dianevallere.com/books